A PLACE TO CALL HOME

By

Darlene Martin

ISBN: 1-4107-0715-6 (e-book)
ISBN: 1-4107-0716-4 (Paperback)
ISBN: 1-4107-0717-2 (Dustjacket)

Library of Congress Control Number: 2002096817

This book is printed on acid free paper.

Printed in the United States of America
Bloomington, IN

1stBooks - rev. 02/10/03

This book is dedicated to my grandmother.
Carrie Belle Street Beavers.
It is her story as she lived it and made it
come alive in my childhood imagination.

AUTHOR'S NOTE

As a child I sat at my grandmother's feet and listened to stories of an Indiana farm and her family's life there. I heard stories of covered bridges, wagon trains traveling to Arkansas and crossing the Mississippi River on a ferry. My imagination was fueled and I longed to have lived those days with my grandmother. This novel is based partly on those stories and is partly from my imagination. I will leave it to each reader's own desecration to determine which are the stories Grandmother Carrie told and those gleaned from my imagination.

Benjamin and Salina Street, their children and their spouses and grand children, Salina's parents Andrew and Emerine Jones and their children Fernando and Jessie, Polk and Mrs. Crabtree and Dick and Effie Beavers and their sons Bill and Don, also Dave and Margaret Grubbs and Charlie Darnell, were real people.

All other persons mentioned in this novel are fictitious and bear no resemblance to anyone living or dead.

The descendants of Benjamin and Salina that it has been my privilege to meet and know all possess common traits and characteristics. All share a love of family and home, an interest in increasing their knowledge and education. They exhibit an interest in science, a love of animals and are interested in animal welfare. They are interested in the Art's whether in the form of music, dance, painting and literature. Many of them are engaged in the fields of engineering, medical fields, some are ministers, many are teachers whether in the academic setting or in schools of dance. Many have served their country in the military during peacetime and in time of war, from Benjamin's service during the Civil War to the present day. Descendants this family are part of the American adventure.

Benjamin and Salina Street
Carrie and Lillie

INDIANA
ONE

Life on an Indiana farm as the nineteenth century was drawing to a close followed a routine as predictable as the changing of the seasons. Carrie's life followed that routine and at the age of thirteen she felt secure and happy. But her life was about to change in ways that she could never have imagined. These changes would alter the course of her life. Her ability to adapt to these changes at such an early age would prepare her for the hardships and trials she would face later in her life. The courage and strength she developed now would sustain her throughout the ninety years of her life.

Carrie and Lillie sat daydreaming and listening to the creak of the wagon's wheels and it rolled along the dusty Indiana road in the warm afternoon sun. It was early spring and the day had been spent in town visiting with their older sisters, Mag and Nellie and their nieces Clara and Mamie. Clara and Mamie were so close in age to Carrie and Lillie they were more like cousins than aunt and nieces.

They had visited with their other sisters Mary and Lottie also. With the help of Uncle Dave Grubbs and his wife Margaret, Mary and Lottie had found jobs and were living with different families. They received a small salary and room and board in exchange for helping the lady of the house with housework and care of the children. Carrie and Lillie missed them and were excited when they were allowed to visit them.

Mary was beautiful and her kindness had always drawn people to her. Lottie was a very quiet and caring person.

Both, Mary and Lottie had suitors who called on them on weekends when they had free time. Mary's suitor was Floyd Caniff. Floyd was a good-looking young man with a good future.

Lottie's young man was Ollie Belcher, who still lived on his father's farm near Oatsville. Although no dates had been set for their marriage, Salina knew it would not be long before two more of her daughters were married.

Carrie's daydreaming was interrupted when she heard her mother and father speak of leaving Indiana.

"But Benjamin, we would have to leave Mary and Lottie here. They have made their lives here. Mag and Nellie are already living in Oatsville. They would never be able to come visit and our grandchildren will grow up without knowing us."

Carrie felt a fear in her heart she had never known before and she nudged Lillie with her elbow. Lillie looked at Carrie, who nodded her head toward the front of the wagon. Lillie focused her attention on the conversation between her mother and father and immediately knew why Carrie looked so worried. Neither of them spoke but listened carefully as their mother and father spoke in low voices.

"Ben, I just don't think we should leave Indiana at our ages and start over. I know you have always wanted to go west. I have lived in Gibson County all my life. I know most of my family have passed on now, but we still have children here. John isn't well. What if there are no doctors there."

"Salina, you know I would not take you to a wilderness where there are no doctors. I have talked to several men who have visited Arkansas and now live there. They tell me the winters are shorter there and there isn't the heavy snowfall that we get here in Indiana. Also, they don't have tornados like we do here. Perhaps the milder climate will improve John's condition. There are hills but not great mountains and the rivers are so clear and pure you can drink from them. Well, enough talk about it for now, but please think about it. Crops have not been good for the last three years and they will have to be extra good this year to meet the mortgage payment."

Fear gripped the young sisters. They had not known there was a mortgage on their home and that they had so little money.

They rode on in silence, each of them lost in their own thoughts. Benjamin was filled with hope and eager for a fresh start. Salina filled with fear and loneliness. Carrie was uncomfortable with all the changes it could bring to her life. Lillie's ambivalent feelings were a mixture of apprehension and excitement.

Carrie was more like her mother. She needed the familiarity and structure of a stable routine. Lillie was more like her father. She liked a challenge and the excitement of not knowing what tomorrow might bring. As the wagon bounced along the dusty road, not one of them knew what hardships and great adventures lay ahead for them.

Drought had come to Indiana for the last three years and this summer had been unusually hot and dry. Benjamin along with the help of his sons, John, Will and Charlie had hauled water form the pump and creek to irrigate the fields. The oats and corn were not producing as good a crop as would be needed. Benjamin's corps were better than most of his neighbors. Those same neighbor's who had laughed and called him "Crazy Benny" for hauling water to his fields, now had almost no crops left with which to feed their families.

As late summer approached, Benjamin realized it was now time for a change. He had not discussed the subject of leaving Indiana with Salina since last spring. He knew she was still uncomfortable with the change it would bring to her life. But Benjamin was a progressive thinking man and knew the future in Indiana would bring changes she would not be comfortable with either.

Benjamin left the hauling of water to his sons and went home early, hoping to find Salina alone so they could talk. The decisions they were about to make would affect not only them but their entire family as well.

Benjamin stopped on the back porch to wash up and stamped the dust from his feet before he entered the house. He found Salina sitting at the sewing machine with yards of pale blue Broadcloth spread on the bed. She was sewing dresses for Carrie and Lillie.

Benjamin moved Salina's sewing basket from a chair and sat next to her. Benjamin was a direct man who did not believe in putting off unpleasant subjects. He knew Salina would know he had serious business on his mind to be home in the middle of the afternoon. Benjamin came right to the point.

"Salina, have you given any more thought to homesteading in Arkansas." Benjamin saw the troubled look in Salina's eyes and waited for her reply.

Salina had thought much about leaving Indiana in the last few months but had hoped it would not come to pass. Now as Ben bought up the subject again Salina grew more concerned.

As Benjamin waited for her to answer, he knew if she were totally against leaving he would never ask her to leave.

"Benjamin, I know things are bad for us financially now and although our crops are fairly good, we won't be able to meet the mortgage payment. I have never liked to owe money for any thing, especially mortgages on our land. I also know if we lost the land to the bank it would break your heart. If it meant making the mortgage payment or caring for our family you would lose the land. If we can sell the land for enough money to pay the mortgage and have enough to travel to Arkansas and build a house when we get there, I suppose it would be best for us. But, I refuse to live in a shanty. You see, I have talked to people about Arkansas, too."

Benjamin smiled and kissed Salina on the forehead. He knew her practical side would overrule her sentimental side. He did not consider the decision a victory over Salina, but a joint decision that would improve their lives and those of their children.

"Have you talked to any of the children yet?" Salina asked.

"No, I wanted us to make a decision before we talked to the them about leaving. I think Lillie and Carrie are suspicious. One day Lillie asked if I ever thought about leaving Indiana. I told her that some day we might want to leave. I know if Lillie is suspicious then she and Carrie will have talked about it. Those two never keep any secrets from each other."

Benjamin returned to the field to help with irrigating the crops. Salina returned to her sewing, but her thoughts were troubled at the prospect of leaving her home for some unknown place called Arkansas.

As Carrie helped mama prepare supper that night she sensed a change in the mother's mood. Could it be fear and uncertainty? Carrie knew mama would tell her what was on her mind at the appropriate time and not before, so she asked no questions. Suddenly Carrie remembered that day last spring when she and Lillie had overheard the conversation between mama and dad about homesteading in Arkansas. Could they have talked about moving again? Did Lillie know about this?

Lillie had been playing with her friend Trudy Warner all afternoon. Yesterday Trudy had left a note in the hole in the old oak tree the girls used as a mailbox when they wanted to contact each other. She had asked if Lillie could come over to play this afternoon. Lillie had begged so hard to go, that Carrie had agreed to do her chores and help mama with supper so Lillie could play.

This afternoon while Carrie had been gathering the last of the summer vegetables from the garden, she had seen dad come in from the fields without her brothers. It was unusual for him to be home in the middle of the afternoon if there was work to be done. Carrie wondered what had made him do so.

"Mama, is something wrong with dad." Carrie asked.

"No Carrie, Why do you ask?"

"I saw him come in from the fields early today, now he has gone back to help the boys finish watering the fields."

"Your father will tell you about it tonight when he tells everyone else." Salina replied. Carrie knew she would have to be satisfied with that answer, for her mother would not disclose any further information until all the family could be included in the discussion. Carrie had finished setting the table when Lillie came home, her face flushed with excitement.

"Mama, guess what Trudy told me today." Lillie said

"I'm sure I have no idea, Lillie but I have a feeling you are about to tell me." Salina said with a smile.

"Trudy said there is a wagon train going to Arkansas in September and the Mercer family is going to move there. Isn't that exciting. It must be wonderful, to go someplace new. There is so much I want to see. I would love to travel all the way to the Pacific Ocean. Last spring we studied about the Pacific Ocean in Geography." Carrie listened as Lillie prattled on and thought, Lillie may get her wish sooner than she knew.

Carrie heard her dad and brothers coming down the lane toward the barn and went to the back porch to ring the dinner bell. She knew it would be a while before they were ready to eat. Dad always insisted that his animals be cared for before they were let out to pasture for the night. Charlie went to the milkhouse to gather milk buckets and would milk the cows before coming in for supper. Dad, Will and John were grooming the horses and throwing hay down from the hayloft and filling the feeding bins with oats and grain.

When chores were finished. Carrie and Lillie waited on the back porch with kettles of hot water for the men folk to wash up before supper. Charlie brought the milk into the milk house where mama would strain and separate the cream from the milk before storing it in large stone jars. The cream would be churned into butter to be sold in town on market day.

As everyone gathered around the large oak table, talk centered around the activities of the day. Carrie noticed dad and mama were unusually quiet, but were listening to the conversations exchanged between their children.

"Will, are you taking Evie Thomas to the dance on Saturday?" Lillie asked.

Before Will could answer, Charlie started teasing him saying, "You know Will never goes anywhere without Evie. Looks like there will be another wedding in this family soon."

Will was good-natured about the teasing, but he was not about to let his younger brother know he had already asked Evie to be his wife. He had planned to talk with her father on Sunday after church services.

Will was a quiet, easygoing young man. He loved to read and spent a lot of his time reading books on Philosophy and the Classics. He was also interested in politics and government, history and geography. These traits were in strict contrast to his younger brother. Charlie liked a good time, was a teaser and at the age of fifteen, very interested in girls. All Girls.

Will considered himself lucky to have been accepted by a young woman as wonderful as Evie Thomas and would devote his life to her. He hoped someday Charlie would settle down with a wife and perhaps live close by.

John was more like Will, quiet and studious. At the age of fifteen a tree limb had fallen and struck him in the head. He was unconscious for several hours. Since that time he had "fits" occasionally. These occurred when he was ill with a fever or under a great deal of stress. Will and Charlie tried to protect John and make things easier for him, but

John was not one to shirk his duties and continued to carry his share of the chores.

As the meal ended, Carrie and Lillie rose to clear the table. Mama said, "Carrie, Lillie, wait a minute. Dad has something to discuss with everyone."

Carrie and Lillie looked at one another and knew this was a turning point in their lives.

Benjamin lit his pipe and hesitated before speaking. You all know as well as I, that because of the drought the past three years and again this year our crops will not earn enough money to pay the mortgage payment and have enough left over to live on for the next year. The time has come for us to make a decision about what is best for the family. Your mother and I have talked about this and know if we stay on here we may lose the farm and not be able to provide for you children.

Will and Charlie exchanged worried looks and spoke almost at the same time. "Dad we could hire out and work on some of the neighboring farms."

"Most of our neighbors are worse off than we are and would not be able to pay you wages." Benjamin replied.

"Then we could go to Evansville and get jobs or go to work in the mines. We can get sleeping rooms there and send you and mama most of our money." Charlie said

"I appreciate what you boys are saying. But that would only be a temporary solution. What we need is a fresh start some place where we can get land cheap and not have a mortgage."

John who had said little thus far spoke up. "I have heard of a wagon train going to Arkansas in September. Some of the men were talking about it when I was in the general store last weekend. So far two families are going and plan to leave the first Monday in September."

Lillie spoke in an excited voice. "Yes, Trudy Warner told me today the Mercer family was leaving in September, but they are poor. How can they have money to travel? It must be wonderful to travel and see new places. Oh! Dad, can we go? I would so love to see new places."

"Well, little daughter your mother and I have talked about homesteading land in Arkansas. The land is free and you just have to live there for seven years and improve it and then it becomes yours."

"How can you improve land?" Lillie asked.

Benjamin laughed. "You live on it, build houses and farm the land. Then after seven years it becomes yours."

"Oh! Dad please can we go? I really want to travel someplace new."

"Well, it looks as if one member of this family is ready for an adventure."

Lillie was almost ten years old and already a beauty like her older sister Mary. But, unlike Mary, Lillie had an adventuresome sprite and loved the thrill of the unknown. From a very early age Mary had always known she wanted a home and marriage with her family near by.

Carrie preferred the familiarity of stable surroundings. She needed the comfort of a daily routine. She needed to know when she awoke in the morning her world would be the same. She was sure she was not going to like this new adventure.

Charlie, like Lillie had an adventuresome spirit and was beginning to like the idea of traveling in a wagon train. This could turn out to be fun.

Benjamin turned to his two older sons. “John, Will, you haven’t said anything yet. What are your thoughts about homesteading?”

Will had always respected his father, but had been taught to value his own thoughts and feelings. This had come as a surprise. He, like Carrie, was not sure he was ready for such a drastic change in his life.

“I haven’t had time to think about it yet. Have you looked into where land is available? What would it cost to outfit wagons? Would we have enough money to get settled somewhere?” Will questioned his father.

“Will, Mother and I have given this a lot of thought. We haven’t worked out all the details yet. But we wanted to discuss it with you children. This will affect your lives as much as mine and your mother’s.”

“Do Mary and Lottie know about this?” Carrie asked. “Will they come with us? What about Mag and Nellie? Will we ever see them again?”

Salina spoke for the first time since Benjamin had opened the discussion.

“Mag, and Nellie are married and have their families and homes here. If Mary and Lottie choose to come with us or to follow us later that must be their decision. I know things have been bad for us but to lose the land to the bank would be heartbreaking. I doubt if your father or any of us could survive that tragedy. But if we could sell the land for enough money to pay the mortgage, we can have the money from the crops to travel to Arkansas and build a home there.”

Benjamin had known he could count on Salina for support. The discussion continued into the evening with questions asked and plans being made then revised. Carrie and Will had little to say.

Carrie knew her mother's heart was breaking at the thought of leaving the home she loved, where her children had been born, where her friends were and where her mom and dad were buried. But like her mother she knew if the bank took the land her mother and father would be devastated.

Benjamin, Will and Carrie saw the pain in Salina's eyes and knew the ache in her heart. Charlie and Lillie were excitedly planning for the great adventure. John said very little, he felt if he left Indiana he would never see it again.

Will and Charlie lay awake that night, each lost in their own thoughts. Will would see Evie on Saturday, but would he have a chance to talk to her about how this new development would affect their lives? Should he ask her father for permission to marry her? Would she be willing to leave her family and move to Arkansas? Could he ask her to do that? For that matter did he want to live in Arkansas?

Charlie was thinking of what exciting things lay ahead for him. He wondered if the girls in Arkansas were as pretty as the ones in Indiana.

Benjamin and Salina talked long into the night, making plans for the journey and the home they would build in Arkansas. The next few weeks would be busy with harvesting the crops, selling the farm and packing. Salina finally fell asleep but it was not a restful sleep and her dreams were troubled with uncertainty and fear of the unknown.

TWO

Early the next morning Will and Charlie rode to town. The rest of the family followed in the wagon.

"Have you told Mary and Lottie we are going to Arkansas?" Carrie asked.

"Not yet." Dad replied. "We plan to tell them after church tomorrow."

They finished the marketing and stopped by to see Mary and Lottie before going home.

On Sunday the family was seated in the middle row of pews in the little Church. Mary and Lottie came in and sat beside them. Salina enjoyed having so many of her children around her. Her heart grew heavy knowing they would soon be telling them they were leaving. That afternoon Mary and Lottie went with them to visit Mag and Nellie in Oatsville. Salina had brought sliced ham and homemade bread and pies in the basket in back of the wagon. After the meal when the girls rose to clear away the table. Benjamin asked them to wait for a while, and began his announcement that the family would be leaving for Arkansas when the crops were gathered.

"Girls, your Mother and I think it is best for our family if we move to Arkansas and homestead land there."

The four older girls gasped and looked at one another with shocked expressions on their faces.

Benjamin continued, "Our crops are not very good this year and have not been good for the past three years. You know we have a mortgage on the farm. I doubt that the crops will produce enough income to pay the mortgage and we would have nothing to live on for another year. Your mother and I could each homestead eighty acres of land and the three boys can each homestead eighty acres. Or at least Charlie will be able to when he becomes of age at eighteen. It will be a new start for all of us. Starting out with no debts will make for an easier living.

By the time Benjamin had finished speaking the girls had recovered enough to begin asking questions. Nellie was the first to recover but had not heard all that her father had said due to the shock of his announcement.

"Do you agree with this mama?" Nellie asked. "What if you don't like living there, would you come back home?

Mary and Lottie did not speak at first they were so shocked. When Lottie could finally speak she asked, "Mama how can you leave your home? You have lived here all your life. Grandma and grandpa and uncle Jessie are buried here. Uncle Fernando and his family are all that is left of your family. How can you leave them? Mary and I will be married one day and have families. We would never see you. Mag and Nellie already live here in Oatsville but at least we can see them occasionally. With you away in Arkansas we would never see you."

Finally Mary was able to speak. "I really don't want you to move so far away. Why Arkansas? What about somewhere closer? Grandma Emerine came from Kentucky. Isn't there still land available for homesteading there?"

"The land that is still available in Kentucky is near the Missouri and Tennessee borders and from all reports isn't very productive land. I have investigated all the land around close and there just doesn't seem to be anything to compare with what is available in Arkansas."

"I am going to miss my family." Lottie said. "But I know mother and dad have given this a lot of thought and would not be making these changes if they didn't believe it was best for their family. Besides we can take the train and go for visits. They do have trains in Arkansas don't they?"

They talked long into the afternoon making plans and discussing when they would leave, the route they would travel and making plans for visits and promises to write letters and send pictures.

Will had not been with the family. He had spent the afternoon with Evie. He had planned to ask her father for permission to marry her, but felt his life was too uncertain now. After church he had walked Evie home and had been invited to eat dinner with her family.

After the meal he and Mr. Thomas had discussed the weather and crops, while Evie had helped with the dishes and cleaning the kitchen. As she entered the parlor, Will rose to his feet and asked, "Would you like to go for a walk Evie?

"I will get my fan. It is so hot this afternoon." Evie was back in a few minutes. They said good-by to her parents and walked down toward the center of town. Will was unusually quiet. After a while Evie spoke. "Will, did you talk to papa about us getting married?"

"No, not yet. I needed to talk to you first Evie. Things have changed since we talked about marriage."

Evie had noticed the strange tone in Will's voice and noticed his withdrawn manner as they had walked home from church, but knew Will would tell her nothing until he felt the time was right. "What things have changed? You still want us to be married don't you?"

"Dad and mama are moving to Arkansas and I have to go with them to help them get moved and settled. I can't ask you to go with us. That would be to great a hardship for you. I couldn't ask you to endure that."

"You still want us to be married don't you? I would marry you and go with you." Evie said.

"You know I want us to be married, Evie." The pain and anxiety were evident in his voice. "But it will be a long hard trip traveling in covered wagons. I don't know how long it will take to get there. I am not even sure what we will find when we get there. I am not sure I will want to stay in Arkansas. But I will have to help them get moved and settled there."

"Will you speak to father about us getting married before you leave?"

"I don't know. Do you think I should?" Will asked.

"Don't you want us to be engaged?" Evie replied, her indignation evident.

"Evie I want us to be married more than anything, but I want to protect you. No, I don't think we should be married before I leave. But I will speak to your father about our engagement." Will reached out and took Evie's hand. He wanted to kiss her but knew that would not be proper before they were engaged. He would speak to her father this afternoon.

THREE

On Monday morning Benjamin, Will and Charlie went into town. They stopped at the bank where Benjamin discussed the mortgage and selling the farm. Mr. Miller the banker told him of a man who had arrived in town last week and was looking to purchase farmland. He was staying at a boarding house on Seminary Street. Mr. Miller promised to tell the man about Benjamin's farm if the man was still in town.

Next they stopped by the blacksmith shop. They had two wagons but would need another and they would need to fit all three with frames to hold the large canvas tops.

John had stayed home and was checking the crops to see when they would be ready for harvest. It would be early October before the harvest would be finished. If they were late in leaving the weather could be cold before they arrived in Arkansas. John saw evidence that the crops were ripening. But, it would be another three weeks before the harvest could begin.

Mama, Carrie and Lillie began looking through trunks, closets and making a list of things to take with them. The list grew so long mama worried if they would have room for everything in three wagons.

When dad and the boys arrived home just after noon, Carrie and Lillie were in the orchard where peaches and apples were drying on racks in the sun. The fruit needed to be turned every other day and it was Carries and Lillie's job to see that it was done.

Salina met Benjamin on the front porch. While the boys tended to the horses, Benjamin told Salina what Mr. Miller had told him about a stranger looking for farmland.

"John says the crops won't be ready to start the harvest for another three weeks. By the time we finish won't that make it to late to leave for Arkansas? It would be winter by the time we get there." Salina said.

"Yes, that is a problem I had hoped to avoid. I was hoping to be able to leave sometime in September if possible. But that will depend on how fast the harvesting goes and if the weather is good. I talked to Mr. Mercer today and they are leaving the first Monday in September. It would be better if we could travel with other wagons, but I doubt if we could have everything settled by them. Mr. Mercer has a reputation of being a "nere do well." He talks a lot but says little. It might not be a very pleasant journey traveling with him. There is another young couple by the name of McKay traveling with him. I think Will might know him. He is about Will's age and has a wife and young baby."

"I talked with the blacksmith and we can get another wagon and the other two outfitted for about two hundred dollars. Do you think we can manage everything in three wagons?" Benjamin asked.

"I have begun a list and I doubt if three wagons will hold all the things we need and the things I can't leave behind. Will we have enough money for everything?" Salina asked.

"That will depend on what we can get for the corps and the sale of the farm. I want to have enough to live on for at least two years until we can get land cleared and crops started. It will take longer to get the orchard growing and producing fruit. We will just have to wait and see when we can sell the farm."

John came out of the barn where he had been checking the harness. He had oiled the tack and saddles and taken inventory of the tools. He was making a list of what they would need for the journey and what they would need to get started in Arkansas. As he left the barn he saw a buggy pulling up in front of the house. Two men left the buggy and were walking up to the front porch.

Benjamin came down the front steps to greet them. One was Mr. Miller, the banker Benjamin had talked to this morning. Mr. Miller introduced the other man as Mr. Simmons, the man he had told Benjamin about this morning. Mr. Simmons was from Georgia and was moving his family to Indiana.

Benjamin asked them into the house and introduced them to Salina and Will. Salina rose to leave the room but Benjamin asked her to stay.

Salina called to Carrie and Lillie, who were in the kitchen, to bring lemonade for everyone.

Mr. Miller came right to the point. "Ben, Mr. Simmons wants to buy farmland in this area. I have told him about your farm and he said it sounded like what he was looking for."

Mr. Simmons had not said much, but had been cautiously looking about the house. He was thinking his wife would be very pleased with this house.

He spoke, "Mr. Street may I ask why you want to sell this farm?"

"We have talked of going west and homesteading for sometime now. The last two years have been very hot and dry and crops have not been very good. We just feel this is the time for a change." Benjamin did not feel the need to discuss the mortgage with Mr. Simmons. Salina was glad he did not mention it.

"I saw your crops as we came by the fields, they look very good. At least better than most I have seen so far"

"That's because Ben and his sons have hauled water to irrigate them." Mr. Miller replied.

"That's very interesting." Mr. Miller replied. "Tell me more about how you do this."

"Why don't we go look at the fields and I can show you." Benjamin said.

Will had said little since the men had entered the house. But, he had been listening to the exchanges between the men and began to like what he saw and heard Mr. Simmons say.

They walked toward the barn where John sat oiling and cleaning the tools. Benjamin introduced his eldest son.

"How do you feel about leaving Indiana, John?" Mr. Simmons asked.

"I will go where ever my family thinks it is best for us to live."

"I have three sons. Two of them are married. If I buy land here they will live nearby. I also have three daughters. I think they will like living in Indiana."

Now it was Benjamin's turn to ask questions. "Where are you from Mr. Simmons?"

Mr. Simmons hesitated before answering. "I live in Georgia." He replied.

Now it was Benjamin who hesitated, but then asked. "Why do you want to leave Georgia?"

"Things have not been very good for us there since the war. I don't know how you felt about the war, but I joined the Union army. I did not feel that states should leave the union. I believed that we would be on the brink of disaster and at the mercy of foreign powers if our nation were to be divided. I was sixteen years old when I volunteered in sixty-three. I had already seen many of my family and friends killed or maimed in a war that never should have taken place. I returned home in sixty-five and it was five years before my wife's father would allow us to be married. It's been rough trying to get established there. Especially if you fought for the wrong side."

"Well, you fought for the right side and that was the side to preserve the union." I fought with the Forty Second Indiana Infantry at Chattanooga, Look Out Mountain and marched with Sherman. I don't feel the people of the south should be punished, as some people believe. It's time to heal our wounds and become one nation again."

"I agree with you and progress has been made but I believe it will be a long time before we see that happen."

They had reached the field where Ben had been irrigating. He had a large vat mounted on a wagon and had used boards to build a sluice that reached twenty feet on either side of the vat. There were pipes about four inches in diameter, which were fitted into the sluice about every four feet. The water was hauled in large barrels and poured into the vat. When the vat was full the doors of the sluice were opened to allow the water to run into the pipes and out between the rows of corn and oats. By placing the pipes between every other row you could water a larger area. With the vat mounted on a wagon, it could move it to various areas and water the entire field.

Mr. Simmons was very interested in Ben's irrigation system. They talked on at great length about how to move it from place to place and how many people it took to operate it.

As they walked back to the house Mr. Simmons inspected the barns and milk house. He liked what he saw. Benjamin's animals were well cared for and the house and buildings were in a good state of repair.

They returned to the house where Salina, Carrie and Lillie were preparing supper. No one ever left Benjamin's house hungry. Mr. Simmons and Mr. Miller were asked to stay for supper and accepted the invitation. Conversation centered on the farm, crops and plans for the trip.

After supper Mr. Simmons asked to see the rest of the house. Benjamin showed him around, much to Salina's embarrassment. Salina was very particular about her house and everything was always neat and clean. But she and the girls had been sorting through clothes and things they wanted to take with them. Everything was not in the usual state of orderliness.

Mr. Simmons understood, his wife would have been very irate if had he allowed anyone to see their house when it was not neat and everything in it's place.

There were four bedrooms upstairs. Down stairs there was a large kitchen, a parlor and a large bedroom which Benjamin and Salina shared. After the tour Mr. Miller and Mr. Simmons prepared to leave. Benjamin walked outside with them.

Mr. Simmons asked, "When do you plan to leave?"

"That will depend on when we can sell the farm and harvest the crops." Benjamin replied. "John tells me the harvest can begin in about three weeks and that will take about six weeks to complete. We hope to be able to leave about the first of October."

"Would you be interested in selling the crops in the field if we can come to an agreement on the sale of the farm. It looks as if the crops will bring about eight hundred dollars at market. I would pay you five hundred and harvest them myself. You could leave for Arkansas sooner and not risk the chance of bad weather. I could send a telegram to my family and they could be ready to leave in a week or two. We have already made arrangements to ship our household belongings on the train and my wife, our daughters and son's families will travel by train. My sons will bring the livestock and wagons with them. I could hire someone to help with the harvest if it is ready before they arrive. We haven't discussed the price of the farm yet. How much are you asking for it?"

Benjamin hesitated. He had planned to ask three thousand five hundred for the farm.

"I am asking three thousand five hundred for the farm. I will talk to my family about selling the crop.'

Mr. Simmons spoke again, "I will have to think about that. Why don't you meet me at the bank tomorrow morning at ten-o-clock to see if we can reach an agreement."

They shook hands after agreeing to meet the next morning and Benjamin returned to the house. Salina was coming out of the kitchen.

"Did you come to an agreement with Mr. Simmons?" Salina asked.

"He offered to buy the crops in the field for five hundred dollars. We could leave for Arkansas in early September if he agrees to buy the farm."

This came as a shock to Salina. She was just getting used to the idea of leaving and now Ben was saying they could be gone in less than a month. She was not sure she was ready for such drastic changes in her life.

That night the family gathered around the dining room table, discussions centered on the trip. Which would be the best route? How long it would take to get there and what they would be able to take with them? Only Will and Carrie saw the pain in their mother's eyes and knew the heartbreak she was enduring.

They went to bed that night each involved in their own thoughts and feelings. Will was thinking of Evie and missing her already. Lillie and Charlie were excited about their new adventure. John sat in his room for a long time thinking how this was changing his life. He thought about the farm he had known all his life. Every inch of it was imbedded in his memory. He took out his autograph book and read the entries written by his friends. Some had written, "Forget me not." He was sure he never would. Benjamin and Salina talked quietly as they prepared for bed. Carrie lay on her bed in the room she shared with Lillie. Her heart ached and tears slid silently down her cheeks.

The next morning Will, Charlie and Benjamin went to town. John had been asked to go but had wanted to stay home. He had gone to the barn and began sorting and packing the tools.

Salina, Carrie and Lillie were sitting at the kitchen table drinking tea and unsure just where to begin with the packing.

Lillie was less enthusiastic about the move this morning. She had heard Carrie crying in her sleep last night. She looked across the table and saw the ache in he mother's eyes.

"Don't worry Mama. Things will be good for us in Arkansas. We will make them good for you."

Lillie rose, walked around the table, placed on arm around her mother and one around Carrie. They stood for several minutes, their hearts and souls bonding together, sharing the pain and loss of leaving all that was dear and familiar to them. Each of them silently vowing never to let Benjamin know how much pain they were feeling.

Benjamin went to the bank while Will and Charlie went to the blacksmith shop to check on the wagons. Inside the bank Mr. Miller and Mr. Simmons waited. Greetings were exchanged and the men got down to the business of the sale of the farm.

"Mr. Street I'm prepared to meet your price if you are willing to leave the irrigation equipment."

This was agreeable to Benjamin. He had planned to leave the irrigation equipment since it was too large to transport such a long distance. They signed the papers, shook hands, Benjamin deposited the money in his account and left to find his sons.

Mr. Simmons went to the telegraph office to wire his family they had a new home.

When Benjamin left the bank he walked to the blacksmith shop where he met Mr. Mercer. He was talking to the blacksmith about his wagons.

Benjamin told him he was planning to travel to Arkansas and homestead land. They talked for a time about which routes to take and how long the trip would take.

Mr. Mercer said, "Travel light. Don't take anything heavy like cook stoves, furniture or wash kettles, only the bare essentials. I plan to travel twenty-five miles per day and seven days a week. I figure I can get there in four weeks. I am going to leave the first week of September. You are welcome to travel with me but you will have to do things my way. I won't have any stragglers holding me back."

"Well, it looks as if you will have to go without me. I won't push my family and animals to the point of exhaustion. My wife and I are older. This move is hard enough on her without pushing so hard. I won't travel on Sunday. My family and livestock will need a day of rest. I would rather take a little longer and not be worn out when we get there. We will need to get our home built before winter."

Benjamin was short of stature, standing only five feet six inches tall. He had came from Switzerland at the age of six with his parents and seven brothers and sisters. His parents had died on board ship coming over. His older brothers and sisters had placed the four younger ones with different families and had gone back to Switzerland. The family with whom he had lived had not treated him very well. He had learned at an early age to defend and care for him self. His spunk had not decreased with age.

Just then young Aaron McKay came into the blacksmith shop. Mr. Mercer introduced him to Benjamin.

"I know your son Will, Mr. Street. We have played baseball together several times. Are you going to Arkansas too?" Aaron McKay asked.

Mr. Mercer answered for Benjamin. "Ben was asking my advice about the trip to Arkansas."

Benjamin was annoyed that Mr. Mercer would answer for him, but held his temper in check. "We are planning to leave about the first of September if the wagons can be ready by then."

"My wife and I are planning to travel with Mr. Mercer. We only have one wagon. Why don't you join us? It would be safer with more wagons." Aaron McKay replied.

Mr. Mercer spoke up again. "Ben and I have different ideas about how to travel. He wants to rest on Sunday and travel slower to coddle his animals. I say we need to move as fast as possible before we have bad weather."

Benjamin held his anger again and spoke to Aaron McKay. "If we take a little longer and take care of the animals we will arrive in better condition to start building homes. Our families will tolerate the trip better. No, it makes more sense to me to pace ourselves and not be exhausted when we arrive."

Aaron McKay had already committed himself to travel with Mr. Mercer but was having second thoughts about the trip. He believed it would be better to go with Benjamin Street, but would wait and see what happened.

Mr. Mercer was a shrewd and calculating man. He knew he could coerce young Aaron McKay to go along with his way of thinking. But Benjamin Street was another matter. He knew Benjamin would not be leaving Indiana if he had not sold his farm and would have enough money to get settled in Arkansas. It could be to his advantage to go along with Ben. If they had trouble along the way perhaps he could borrow money from Ben. His own funds were very limited. He had no property to sell and only had the money from the sale of his few head of livestock and household furnishings. Yes! It might be better to go along with Ben after all.

"You know you might be right Ben. If we could leave the last week of August that would give us another week and traveling slower would be better for my family, too.

Young McKay has one wagon. I will have two and with your three we would have a larger wagon train and travel would be safer. My son Jamie is fifteen and handles a team real well and my wife can handle a team too."

Benjamin was not fooled by Mr. Mercer's apparent change of heart. But, knew it would be safer to travel together. He also knew Aaron would have to do all the dirty work for Mr. Mercer and if they got into trouble Aaron would be left alone to cope with the difficulty.

"If we can come to some agreement on the rules of travel I will go with you, but I won't push my family or my animals to the point of exhaustion just to save time."

Aaron McKay agreed with Ben and Mr. Mercer finally agreed to do things Ben's way. The Blacksmith said the wagons would be ready in two weeks. They planned for one week to pack and load and secure provisions. Benjamin planned to carry plenty of food, for they would not pass through towns with markets for days at a time. They agreed to meet the following Saturday at Benjamin's to discuss plans and for the families to get acquainted.

After this was settled Ben went to look for his sons. He found Charlie at the general store looking at rifles.

"Dad I think we need another gun, I know you have your pistol and shotgun, but we could use a rifle to hunt for game and for protection."

"Yes, Charlie we do need another gun. I believe we could use two. Each wagon will need a weapon and my pistol is so old it is hard to find ammunition for it. I will take the shotgun on our wagon and Will and John can take the rifles." Charlie picked out two rifles. He felt a little slighted that Ben had not assigned one of the guns to him. But, he knew that if he needed one Will or John would loan it to him. Benjamin ordered the rest of the supplies on Salina's list and they were ready to start for home.

"Where is Will?" Benjamin asked.

"He went to see Evie. I don't think he wants to leave her. He has hinted about their being engaged. But, you know Will. He won't say anything until he thinks it's the right time."

Ben had known Will was getting serious about Evie. She was a lovely girl from a good family and would be a devoted wife. But he was counting on Will settling in Arkansas near him. Perhaps he should talk to Will about his plans. Maybe on the way home he would bring up the subject.

They finished gathering their provisions, loaded the wagon and were about to start home by way of Evie's house, when they saw Will coming down the street. Will climbed into the wagon and the three headed home. The sun was setting as the crossed the covered bridge and it was almost dark as they passed the Wheeling Schoolhouse. Will was very quiet on the way home and neither, Ben or Charlie brought up the subject of Evie Thomas.

Supper was waiting when they arrived home. After the animals had been taken care of, they went into the house. They were met with a lot of questions. Everyone wanted to know everything at once. As they ate, Benjamin explained all about the terms of the sale and his conversation with Mr. Mercer and young Aaron McKay.

"Aaron says he knows you, Will. He has a wife and young baby. They will be traveling with us. He seems like a good worker and a nice young man."

"He is a very honorable young man and if he gives his word you can count on it. I am glad he will be traveling with us. Although I am not sure Mr. Mercer will be much help. He has a reputation of not being dependable."

Will changed the subject. "I want to talk to the family about mine and Evie's plan's. We are going to be married but not until we get settled in Arkansas. I will come back for her after I can get a house built there."

Everyone was excited about Will's news and conversation flowed around the table with congratulations and discussion of wedding plans.

The rest of the week was spent sorting the things they were planning to take with them and what would be sold or left with the farm. Benjamin and his sons continued to irrigate the fields. There still had been no rain and it was the beginning of the second week of August.

FOUR

On Saturday just after noon, Mr. Mercer and Aaron McKay arrived with their families. Introductions were made. Salina and Carrie served tea and cake.

The conversation switched from the usual topics to travel plans. Benjamin and the men folk walked out to the barn to inspect the wagons and livestock.

Mrs. Mercer was a frail little woman who looked much older than her years. "Mrs. Street, your home is so nice how can you bare to leave it?"

"Mrs. Mercer, please call me Salina. Yes, it is hard for me to leave my home. I have lived in Gibson County all my life. I have grown and married daughters and grandchildren who will be left here. Benjamin has always talked of going west. We are getting older. If we don't go now we may not have another chance."

"You must call me Abigail, Salina. My James has always talked of going to Arkansas. He thinks things will be better for us there. But I know our life will be what we make of it where ever we are."

Beth McKay had sat quietly as the women talked. She liked both of the older women. She thought Salina Street was much like she remembered her own mother. Beth's mother had died when she was ten years old and she had been passed from one relative to another until she had married Aaron. Now that she was a mother herself she was determined to provide her baby with the best home she could. She liked Mrs. Mercer, but did not care for Mr. Mercer. She was glad they would be traveling with the Street family.

Mrs. Mercer had two children. Her son Jamie was fifteen years old and her daughter Emily was eight years old. Emily was a scrawny little girl who was pretty in spite of being so thin. She had blond hair, which had a natural curl around her face.

Jamie was tall for his age and was entering puberty. His voice was changing and at times when he spoke had a high-pitched squeak. He had pimples on his face. He kept trying to get Carrie's attention by acting a fool. Carrie was not impressed. As a matter of fact, she thought he was revolting, but was trying hard to be polite. All the while she was wishing he had gone to the barn with the men.

Lillie and Emily were soon talking like old friends. Lillie had brought the kittens from the barn and both girls sat on the ground with a lap full of kittens. Carrie joined them and began to pet the kittens and ignored Jamie. He finally became discouraged with trying to get her attention and wandered out to the barn and began talking to John.

After awhile the men returned from the barn and the conversation returned to plans for the trip. The blacksmith had promised the wagons would be ready next Saturday. They would take a week to pack and load everything. Benjamin's home was the closest place to start the trip. It was decided they would leave on Monday morning. Everyone agree with that.

Salina could not believe that in two weeks she would be leaving her home. She smiled as she said good-by to Beth McKay and Abigail Mercer.

As they walked into the house Carrie asked dad if they could take the cats and their kittens.

"We can't take them all Carrie, but you and Lillie can each take one cat and her kitten's and we will take King.

King the family dog, was part Collie and well over ten years old. He was very much a part of the family. As a pup John had trained him to work the cattle. He and John were constant companions.

The next week flew by in a flurry of activity. Lillie and Carrie packed the dried peaches and apples in clean white flour sacks to be stowed in the large barrels John had washed, scalded and that were now drying in the sun. Salina was packing dishes and her vases in her mother's old steamer trunk. She packed the family pictures in the trunk also. These were things she could not leave behind. Benjamin had promised to buy her a new cook stove when they got to Arkansas. She knew the old one was to heavy to transport so far, but she hated to sell it. She had insisted on taking her Singer sewing machine and Ben had given in on that.

John was packing the tools and harness while Benjamin, Will and Charlie continued to irrigate the crops.

On Saturday all the family went to town. Salina had a list of provisions she would need for the trip. She bought ointments, liniments and muslin for bandages in case of injuries to the family or animals. She bought tea, coffee, beans, flour, cornmeal, sugar, oatmeal and lard. Their supply of meat was low and the weather was still too warm to butcher. There was still one ham and one side of bacon left in the smokehouse. They would replenish the meat supply as they passed through the towns along the way or hunt for wild game.

While Salina and the girls were shopping, John, Charlie and Benjamin went to the blacksmith shop to check on the wagons. Will went to see Evie.

When her shopping was finished Salina went to visit with her friends and to say good-by. Some were excited and anxious to hear about her trip. Others were critical and could not believe at her age she was leaving her home and traveling to a wilderness called Arkansas. They all asked her to write and said they would miss her. Many of her friends she had known since childhood. She wondered if she would ever have friends like these again.

At four-o-clock they met at the blacksmith shop. Benjamin had paid his account at the general store and picked up the provisions Salina had bought. He had also settled his accounts at the bank. The wagons they had driven into town were now fitted with a frame and huge canvas cover. Salina wasn't sure she would be able to pack everything she wanted to take with her in three wagons.

As they started for home Will drove one wagon and John rode with him. Charlie drove the smallest of the three wagons with Carrie and Lillie riding in the back. Benjamin and Salina drove the other. The sun was setting as they reached home. Salina and the girls went into the kitchen and started fixing supper while Benjamin and the boys tended to the stock and unloaded the supplies.

Salina was just setting supper on the table when Charlie came running in from the barn yelling for her.

"Mama, come quick. It's John. He's having one of his fits."

Salina ran to the barn where she found Benjamin and Will holding John in their arms while his body jerked in uncontrollable motions. Salina knew this seizure was much worse than any he had ever had before. Will was cradling him and trying to keep his body from hitting anything that could injure him. Benjamin was holding his arms and lying across his legs to try to hold him. Will was calling his name in a soft soothing voice. Blood tinged saliva ran from his mouth. Salina asked for Ben's handkerchief and rolled it in to a tight roll and placed it between John's teeth to prevent him from biting his tongue. After what seemed an eternity but was in reality only a few minutes, Salina saw John's body stiffen in to a clonic state and knew the seizure was about over and John would sleep for awhile. After a few minutes in the clonic state John's body began to relax. Will and Charlie carried him up to his room. Lillie and Carrie met them at the door and carried warm water and towels up to John's room. Salina bathed his face and hands. Benjamin and Will undressed him and covered him with a sheet. While John slept Salina sat by his bed. Ben, Will and Charlie went downstairs to eat supper. But no one felt much like eating. For the first time Benjamin wondered if moving to Arkansas was the right thing to do. What if the stress of moving were to much for John?

As they went to their room Carrie and Lillie looked in John's room and saw mama sitting by John's bed. They quietly went to their room, closed the door, held each other and cried.

Salina sat by John's bed all night as he slept. As dawn was breaking she dozed in the chair. John stirred and Salina was immediately aroused.

"This was a bad seizure, mama. But I felt it coming. I had seen flashes of bright light several times today and while we were feeding the stock everything looked hazy with a light behind it."

"You must tell someone if you ever have those feelings again. Maybe we can do something to stop the seizure."

"I don't know if we can stop them but I could lay down so I would not fall." John said.

Salina went downstairs where Carrie and Lillie were already preparing breakfast.

"How is John this morning?" Carrie asked.

"He's better this morning and he slept through the night. This is the worst seizure he has ever had. He told me he had warnings this time. He saw flashes of light several times today and had visions of hazy figures with a light behind them,"

"Does this mean his condition is getting worse?" Lillie asked.

"I hope not, but at least if he has warnings he can protect himself." Salina replied.

The men folk came in from the barn and were told of John's condition this morning.

John was coming down the stairs dressed and ready for breakfast. After breakfast and chores were done they left for church service. This was to be the last service they would attend in the little church where Salina had grown up. Today she would be saying good-by to another part of her life. Sometimes she wished they were already gone and these painful farewells were behind her.

As they entered the church they saw Mary and Lottie sitting with Floyd and Ollie in the last pew from the back of the church. They moved over and the family slid in beside them. Will went to where Evie was sitting and sat next to her. After the sermon the pastor announced this was the last service the Street family would be in attendance. They were leaving next week. After the services, friends gathered around to say good-by. Will went home with Evie to spend the afternoon. The rest of the family went home to a light lunch and rested for the remainder of the afternoon.

Monday morning they began to pack and load the wagons. Very little of the furniture would be taken. Benjamin preferred to carry enough provisions for the trip, so most of the space in the wagons would be filled with barrels of food. He would purchase household necessities when they had a home built.

The sewing machine and trunks were loaded first, then the barrels of food and supplies. Mattress and feather beds were loaded last. By Friday the wagons had been loaded and reloaded so that everything was neatly and efficiently arranged. Cooking utensils were easily accessible as well as the axes, which would be needed to cut firewood. Two of the wagons would carry the new rifles and Benjamin would have the old pistol and shotgun with him. The furniture and other belongings were to be sold tomorrow.

Mr. Simmons and his family arrived early Saturday, so Mrs. Simmons could see the house. She was a friendly woman and Salina liked her immediately.

Mrs. Simmons liked the house and began to make plans for curtains and spreads and where she would place her furniture. Salina felt pangs of resentment that another woman would be living in her home. She hid these feelings as she showed Mrs. Simmons around the house.

Mrs. Simmons liked the large oak dining room table and chairs and decided to buy them right away. She bought several others pieces of furniture as well as the large cook stove. Mr. Simmons bought most of the tools. They had been well cared for and would be needed for the harvest. His sons would arrive next week with the livestock and wagons. The crops would be ready to harvest soon after that. Benjamin and his sons had done a good job of irrigating and he looked forward to a good harvest.

By three-o-clock, everything had been sold, except the things Benjamin and Salina were giving to Mag, Nellie, Mary and Lottie.

Salina cooked her last meal on the large cast iron stove and served it on Mrs. Simmons dining table. She felt so strange, as if she were in someone else's home instead of her own. The beds had been sold so that night they slept on mattress on the floor.

On Sunday morning Mary and Floyd, Lottie and Ollie and Mag and Nellie and their families arrived to spend the day. They brought food for lunch and supper. The day was spent in visiting and the children played games. As the sun began to set, tearful good-bys were exchanged and the older girls and their families left for their homes. Their hearts were heavy as they wondered how long it would be before they saw their mother and father, brothers and sisters again.

No one slept much that night. Each one was lost in thought. Each one was trying to sort out their emotions. Will was thinking of Evie and wondered if he had the right to ask her to wait for him. How long would it be before he saw her again? John felt he would never again see the home and farm he loved. Benjamin and Salina hoped they were not making a mistake by taking their family so far away. Charlie was filled with anticipation for what this new adventure might mean to his life. Lillie was filled with excitement to be going some place new. Carrie felt a fear of the unknown, but felt a trust in her father, that he would always be there to take care of her.

They were up at daybreak the next morning and had just finished eating breakfast when Mr. Mercer and Aaron

McKay arrived with their wagons. Everyone, except Salina and Carrie, was eager to get started. Salina had gone for one more look around the house. Carrie and Lillie were nowhere to be seen. John went to the barn where he found them trying to decide which of the cats and their kittens to take with them.

"It's time to go girls." John said.

"But we can't leave the kittens. What if Mr. Simmons' daughters don't like cats." Lillie cried.

"Mr. Simmons said his family likes cats and he likes them in the barn to keep mice out of the feed."

"You take Muffin and her kittens and I'll take Bitsy and her babies." Carrie said. They petted and cuddled the other cats and kittens, and told them good-by. Then they took Bitsy and Muffin and their kittens to the back of Will's wagon. John called to King, who came running from the oat field and the little group boarded the wagons. John was to drive the smallest of the wagons and King jumped up onto the wagon and sat on the seat beside him. Will drove one of the large wagons. Carrie, Lillie and the cats rode with him. Benjamin and Salina were in the other wagon. Charlie would ride the extra horse and watch the four head of cattle they were taking with them. Two of the cows had calves with them, but the calves would follow their mothers and would be no problem.

Mr. Mercer shook his head when he saw all that the Street family was taking with them and thought, "This is going to be some trip."

It was just after seven-o-clock when the wagon train pulled out of the yard and started down the lane. As they rounded the bend in the road everyone, even Charlie looked back with sadness at the home they were leaving. But each of them was taking many happy memories with them.

Just before they reached the covered bridge they met Mr. and Mrs. Simmons with their wagons heading for the farm. They stopped for a few minutes to exchange good luck wishes and good-bys and then started on. Although Carrie would move many times in her life, no move would ever be as painful or evoke the sense of loss she felt as she left her home in Indiana.

THE JOURNEY
FIVE

The wagons rolled along with Mr. Mercers two wagons in the lead, Aaron McKay's wagon was next, and the Street wagons were last. Benjamin put some distance between his wagons to allow the dust to settle a little. As they neared town, Will called to Charlie to take the reins of his wagon. He took Charlie's horse and rode into town to say good-by to Evie. John pulled his wagon alongside Charlie's and asked, "Where is Will going?"

"He didn't say but I will bet you money he is going to say good-by to Evie Thomas." Charlie replied. "He will catch up with us soon."

Will rode to Evie's house and knocked on the door. When Evie answered, she was surprised to see him standing there. He entered the house, looked into Evie's eyes and said. "I just couldn't leave with out seeing you again. I'll write to you daily and mail it when we get to a town with a post office.

"I am so glad you came. I will miss you so. How long will it be before you can come back for me?"

"I don't know Evie, but I will come for you as soon as I can." Will kissed Evie for the first time and wished it would not be very long before he could be with her again. Evie walked down the steps with Will and watched as he mounted the horse and galloped down the street.

It was almost eleven-o-clock by the time Will caught up with the wagon train. Benjamin and Salina did not ask Will where he had gone. They knew he had to see Evie one last time.

They rode on for another hour before stopping for the noon hour. They had traveled about ten miles this morning, and everyone still felt the excitement of starting the adventure.

The late August days were still warm so they did not build a fire. Salina cut thick slices of homemade bread she had baked on the big old stove at home. There was cheese she had made and left over bacon from breakfast. After they had eaten Salina put beans in the big iron kettle to soak. She would cook them over a campfire when they stopped for the night. She took tealeaves and tied them in a white cloth and placed them in a large glass jug and filled it with water. Then she sat it in the sun in the back of the wagon. The sun would brew tea while they traveled.

The afternoon went much slower as they settled into a slow pace. Benjamin checked his pocket watch and saw it was almost four-o-clock.

Charlie rode ahead of Mr. Mercer's wagon to search for a campsite. About an hour later he returned to report a small creek just about a mile ahead. Benjamin knew it would take about another hour to get there. Charlie reported this to Aaron and Mr. Mercer. They arrived at the creek just after six-o-clock. Aaron and Will watered and fed their stock while Charlie and John gathered firewood and got the fires started. Mr. Mercer sent Emily to gather firewood while Jamie and Abigail tended to their livestock. Mr. Mercer busied himself in the back of their wagons. Salina began her preparations for supper. She may not have a proper kitchen but she would make sure her family was well fed.

Benjamin sliced ham steaks while Salina put the kettle of beans on the fire to cook. Carrie and Lillie got dried peaches and apples from the barrels where they had packed them only a few days before. Salina cooked dried apples and peaches and made fried pies. She made extras for the noon meal tomorrow.

They had just finished their meal when Aaron came over and asked Benjamin and Will to help him make a swing for his baby. Baby Michael had been fretful all afternoon. The wagon rode so rough and bumpy the infant had not slept.

Benjamin and Will took a rope from their wagon and tied it to Aaron's wagon frame. Then they fastened the rope around the rockers of the cradle and suspended it about four inches off the wagon bed where it could swing free. It was back far enough under the canvas top so the sunlight would not be so hot on the baby. Beth McKay was so pleased and thanked Ben and Will. Benjamin and Will returned to their wagon to find Carrie and Lillie sitting by the fire, each with a lap full of kittens. Emily Mercer had joined them and wistfully petting one of the kittens.

"I wish papa would let me have a kitten. Papa says cats are not useful animals and that people should only keep animals if they are useful. But I would love a kitten so it would be useful to me."

"We could give you one of our kittens." Lillie said as she looked at Carrie. Carrie and Lillie could not imagine what it would be like not to have a cat and kittens and other animals around.

"The kittens are not old enough to be taken away from their mother yet, but you can claim one and when it is old enough to leave its mother you can have it." Carrie said.

Abigail Mercer came over to sit and visit with Salina for a while. She looked very tired. She had driven a wagon most of the afternoon and then cooked supper and cleaned up the dishes. Emily had helped before she came over to play with Carrie and Lillie.

"Mama, Carrie and Lillie said I could have one of the kittens when they are old enough. Do you think papa will let me have a kitten? I would take good care of it and would not let it bother any one."

"I will talk to your papa about it." Abigail promised. But, she had made up her mind Emily would have a kitten. The family had given up everything to make this move because James had wanted to go. Emily could at least have a kitten.

Beth McKay did not join the older women. The baby had been fussy and was finally sleeping in the cradle swing. She had finished her evening meal and had cleaned up the dishes. She had decided to rest before the baby became fretful again. Aaron piled wood on the fire for more light and was oiling and mending his harness.

Benjamin and John had tethered the horses and cattle in an area where they could graze and drink water from the creek. They had decided it was safe enough they would not need to post a guard tonight. Tonight they would rest for there would be times when they would need to stand guard all night.

They bedded down for the night. Benjamin and Salina in their wagon, Carrie and Lillie in Will's wagon with the kittens at the foot of their mattress. Will and Charlie slept on feather beds spread out in the soft grass. John slept in the other wagon with King at his feet. It was the first time Salina could remember having slept without a roof over her head. She finally fell asleep from the exhaustion and excitement of beginning their journey.

The families all slept soundly even though the world around them was strange and different. Even baby Michael McKay slept through the night.

Thus, began the pattern of their days. They would rise early, travel until about five o-clock and make camp for the night. Each night Benjamin would record the events of the day's journey in a journal. He had a weather thermometer he had bought shortly after his discharge from the Union Army and had always recorded the temperature each day. He described the scenery and climate of the countryside they were passing through.

Will wrote to Evie every night describing the day's journey and how much he missed her. John wrote in his diary, his thoughts and feelings about the day's journey.

Michael McKay was less fussy now that he was not being bumped around so much. He liked the swinging notion of the cradle as the wagon rolled along and when his mother sang to him he would laugh and coo.

On the second night they camped on the north edge of Evansville. Benjamin and Will along with Mr. Mercer and Aaron McKay went into town to purchase a few supplies. While the others went to the general store, Will went to mail his letters to Evie. Mr. Mercer went to the local tavern. After Ben and Aaron finished shopping, Benjamin found him there bragging to a group of men about the wagon train he was leading to Arkansas. Benjamin told him it was time to leave for camp and finally convinced him to go. It was dark when they arrived back at camp just as Salina was finishing supper.

Benjamin had bought fresh apples and pears as a treat for the family. After supper Emily came over to visit her kitten. Lillie and Carrie shared their fruit with her as they played with the kittens. Emily had chosen a Calico cat which she named Speckles. She loved to bury her face in the soft furry kitten. Lillie and Carrie were pleased to see her so happy. They wondered what Mrs. Mercer had said to change Mr. Mercer's mind.

They broke camp early the next morning and the girls were soon bored with the monotony of the same routine each day. Carrie and Lillie climbed down from the wagon and ran up along side the Mercer's wagon. Emily climbed down from her wagon and joined them. They walked along laughing and talking.

Jamie Mercer was still trying to get Carrie to pay attention to him, but his dad kept him so busy driving the wagon and caring for the animals, he did not have much time to talk to her. Carrie was thankful that he did not have time to annoy her. She did feel sorry for him because his dad never gave him a chance to have any fun. He and John were becoming friends. John was teaching him how to care for the harness and animals as well as how to tie different kinds of knots. John had even shared some of the entries in his diary with him.

Jamie had never cared much for school and learning, but he could read and write. Now when John and Will talked about foreign countries and other parts of the United States he wished he had studied more. Jamie's mother had always encouraged him to do well in school, but his father had always needed him to help on the farm. His education had suffered greatly. Emily was a bright child who was warm and loving, but her education had been neglected too

School would be starting next week. Carrie wondered what all her friends were doing. Mama and dad had bought some books. Maybe she would look for some tonight and she and Lillie could read to each other in the long afternoons. That night after supper Carrie asked mama and dad if they knew where the books were packed. Charlie groaned when they asked him to help find them.

Will said, "I have some in my wagon you can read. I also have an atlas so you can follow our route. You can read about Arkansas too."

Will and the girls were looking for the books, when Emily came over to play with her kitten. Emily picked out some books to read too. Each afternoon the girls would sit in the back of Will's wagon amid the kittens and read to each other. Abigail Mercer was pleased to see her daughter so happy and making such good friends.

SIX

On Friday of the third week when they stopped for the noon meal, Aaron McKay came to where Salina was preparing lunch for her family.

"Mrs. Street, Beth would like you to come look at baby Michael. He has a fever and won't eat."

Salina left Carrie and Lillie to finish the meal and went to the McKay wagon.

She found Beth holding Michael and bathing his face with cool water. Salina touched the child and could feel that his fever was very high.

"How long has he been sick?" Salina asked.

"When I put him to bed last night he was fine. But this morning he felt so hot and won't eat and has vomited several times. He looks so weak. I don't know what to do for him." Beth cried.

Salina called to Carrie to come over to the McKay's wagon. When she arrived Salina said, "Have the boys build a fire and boil some water in two pots. When the water boils put some dried apples in one and tie some oatmeal in cheesecloth and boil it in the other. When it has boiled for about five minutes take it off the fire and add some sugar to the liquid and let it cool, then bring it to me. While it is cooking bring me some of the tea sweetened with sugar."

Carrie did as her mother instructed and soon brought the tea to Salina. She put tea in baby Michael's water bottle and tried to get him to suck on it. Michael would only take a little at a time.

Benjamin and Aaron went to Mr. Mercer's wagon to tell him baby Michael was sick. "Mr. Mercer, my baby is sick with a fever. I don't want to travel any further today. Mrs. Street is tending him now. I am sorry for the delay, but my baby is to sick to travel any farther."

It was clear that Mr. Mercer was annoyed at the delay. But he knew he had no choice but to wait until the baby was well enough to travel or go on alone. He knew Ben Street would stay behind with Aaron. They would rest and allow the animals to rest while Beth and Salina cared for baby Michael.

Benjamin, Will, Charlie and Mr. Mercer went into to the town of Metropolis to restock their supplies. Will went to mail his letters to Evie. Aaron had given Ben a list and money to purchase his supplies. He did not want to leave Beth and Michael.

John and Jamie found places for the cattle and horses to graze where they would have plenty of grass and water. John set about checking the harness to see how it was holding out. It needed very little repair. He had seen that it was in good shape before they started the trip. He showed Jamie how to oil the leather to make it stronger and keep it from wearing and breaking.

It was the middle of September and they were traveling through southern Illinois. The countryside was just beginning to come alive with the colors of fall. Maple trees were turning every shade of yellow, orange and red. The days were still warm but the nights were beginning to be cooler. They were camped along the Ohio River. Carrie had never seen such a wide river. She had listened to her father tell stories about when he was in the Civil War and had crossed the Ohio and Tennessee Rivers. But she could not imagine how wide the rivers were. She would never forget the beauty of watching the reflections of the sun shimmering on the Ohio River as she and Lillie and Emily sat watching the sun sink below the horizon.

That night the campfire felt warm and cozy as the night chill settled over the camp. They posted a guard that night and kept the campfire burning bright. John would take the first watch with Charlie relieving him at midnight. Then Will would relieve Charlie at four o-clock. Jamie came to sit with John as he took his turn of watch and they talked for hours while the campfire burned. Salina and Beth took turns caring for Michael, encouraging him to drink the sweetened tea, apple water and oatmeal water. Aaron tried to sleep but was unable to do so. He got up and helped Charlie and Will stand their turn at watch.

As the first light of dawn shown in the eastern sky, Michael felt a little cooler and his breathing was not as fast and shallow. Beth held him in her arms and was dozing when Salina went to her wagon to rest for a while. She awoke to the smell of bacon frying and coffee brewing over the campfire as Carrie, Lillie and Abigail Mercer were preparing breakfast for the whole camp. Emily was helping when she could. After they had eaten Salina took plates of food to Beth and Aaron. She gently lifted the sleeping baby from Beth's arms and placed him in the cradle swing where he slept peacefully while Beth and Aaron ate.

Through out the day, every two hours Salina or Beth would arouse Michael and offer him a drink. He was taking more liquids and felt cooler but was still very sick.

Mr. Mercer was restless with the delay but took advantage of the time to go back into town and visit the local tavern. He had not asked anyone to go with him and did not return until well after midnight.

The boys kept watch throughout the night and kept the fire burning high for light and comfort. This night was the coldest they had so far. Benjamin hoped it would not be and early winter.

On Sunday Michael was much better but still looked thin and pale with dark circles under his eyes. His fever had broken during the night and he was taking more fluids without vomiting. Salina and Beth looked tired. Abigail and Carrie took turns taking care of Michael so they could rest.

At noon Salina started to prepare her Sunday dinner. Ben had bought chickens in town on Friday and now he killed and cleaned them. Salina made chicken and dumplings in the huge iron kettle and everyone on the wagon train ate together. A tradition was begun of eating the Sunday noon meal together with everyone contributing something to the dinner. Salina had missed church services with her family and friends. Now the Sunday fellowship helped her through the loneliness.

On Monday Baby Michael was well enough they could resume their journey.

On Thursday of the following week they reached Cairo, Illinois where they would cross the Mississippi River on a ferry. As they made camp for the night Carrie, Lillie and Emily walked down to the bank of the river. They had never seen so much water and could not imagine that much water existed in one place. That night after supper Carrie asked dad to tell them again about when he came to America. Jamie and Emily had come over to sit by the campfire and were entranced as they listened to Benjamin's stories of crossing the ocean on a boat when he was only six years old.

Benjamin had come to America with his parents and seven brothers and sisters. His parents had died on the boat coming across the ocean. His four older brothers and sisters had found homes for the four younger children and returned to Switzerland. Benjamin had maintained contact with his brother Charles and his sisters Margaret and Mary Anna but had never heard from the other children after they returned to Europe. Ben's memories of his older brothers and sisters had dimmed with time. His memories of his father were somewhat vague. He remembered him as a jolly man who had smoked a pipe and loved to tell stories of his home in Germany. Ben could not remember when they had lived in Germany but remembered living in Bern, Switzerland and how secure and happy he had been there. His memories of his mother were stronger and he remembered a gentle woman who nurtured her children and husband with love and guidance.

He remembered the open-air markets and the arcade streets when his mother did her marketing. He also remembered visiting the Bear pits and seeing the Clock Tower and Prison Tower along the main street of the old city. He had hated to leave Bern and after the death of his parents he had longed to return. But as he grew older he realized that it was impossible to return. He was content with the life he and Salina had built.

Benjamin's life had not been as secure and loving after the death of his parents. The family he had been placed with had come from Germany a few years before the Street family. They had provided him with a place to live and food, but little else. His education had been limited to reading whatever books he could borrow or what he learned from his guardian's children. He was a inquisitive child and remembered details well and always wanted to learn more about the world in which he lived. Benjamin was expected to work hard and he did so. He cared for their animals as if they were his own. He talked to the horses as if they could sense his loss and loneliness.

At the age of sixteen with the Civil War beginning Benjamin saw his chance to begin living his life on his own. One day after the noon meal he returned to the fields, tied the horses to the fence and slipped away to join the Union Army and fought in the Civil War until it ended.

After his discharge in 1865 he returned to Indiana but he did not return to the family he had lived with. It was hard to find work but eventually he found a steady job. He met Salina Jones at a church social and knew she was the girl he wanted to marry. After two years he had saved enough money to properly care of her and asked her to marry him. Andrew and Emerine Jones gave their permission and on December 12, 1867 they were married. Salina's parents were older and Salina, Fernando and Jessie were the only children who had lived to be adults. They had eleven children but only those three had survived.

Jessie had been in the Civil War but had not survived as well as Benjamin. He was prone to bouts of melancholy and had never married. He died at a very early age. Andrew and Emerine had lived near Ben and Salina until they died.

Now listening to Ben tell of leaving Switzerland at such an early age, traveling across the ocean, losing his parents and living with strangers, Salina felt guilt and shame about feeling such unhappiness at leaving Indiana.

The children sat entranced as Ben talked of living on a ship for days and seeing nothing but water. Even Jamie Mercer 's imagination was captured by Ben's stories. He decided right then that he would be a sailor and travel the world. His interest in the world was born that night and he would travel much of his life.

That night as Jamie and John stood their watch, Jamie asked John what he wanted to do with his future.

John replied, "My future is the present. I live each day for the pleasure I find in that day. I have no guarantee of another day so I live each day for itself." This conversation made Jamie very uncomfortable and he changed the subject.

They piled more wood on the fire to keep warmer and to provide more light. The next morning they lined the wagons up to board the ferry. Lillie and Jamie were excited about the boat ride. Carrie and Emily weren't sure they wanted to be on such a small boat in the middle of such a big river. It would take most of the day to get all the wagons and livestock across.

Mr. Mercer was the first to board. The ferryboat would hold two wagons and horses and several people at each crossing. It took about an hour to cross to the other side and unload. Then the return trip took another hour. Next was Aaron McKay's wagon and one of Benjamin's with Salina, Carrie and Lillie on board.

When they arrived on the other side the women set about fixing the noon meal. They would eat when Charlie, Will and John arrived with the last of the wagons and livestock. They would travel a few more hours to make up for the delay at the ferry crossing.

SEVEN

After crossing the river they were traveling through the flat Mississippi delta land and the scenery was not as pretty as it had been in the softly rolling hills of southern Indiana and Illinois. By the next Saturday they camped near the St. Francis River. Just after dark they noticed another campfire across the river from their camp.

A short time later, two men came out of the shadows. They were dressed in baggy pants and bright colored vests with bandannas tied around their heads. The younger of the two had a braided whip coiled and tied to his belt. Salina and the girls were frightened. Ben and Will rose from where they were seated near the campfire and went to meet them.

Benjamin was cautious but did not want the men to know he was suspicious of them. "My name is Ben Street. Can I help you?"

"We're the Molondro brothers. Our camp is just across the river. We are heading east and wondered if you could give us some information about the trail to Paducah, Kentucky." the older man said with a strange accent.

"We came from Evansville, Indiana and crossed the Mississippi River at Cairo, Illinois. I can't tell you much about Kentucky." Benjamin said. "We are headed west."

"I see you have six wagons in your train. How many people are with you?" the older man asked.

"There are three families of us." Benjamin said.

Just then Charlie, John and Aaron walked out of the shadows. Each one had a rifle over their arm. They stood across the fire from the intruders but said nothing.

King was under John's wagon and had begun to growl, but made no move toward the strangers.

"Stay King!" John said. King stopped growling but stayed alert to any movement the men might make.

"The dog is well trained. I could use a dog like that. I will buy him from you." the younger man said.

"He's not for sale." John said.

"I would pay you a good price for him." the man continued.

"I said he's not for sale at any price." John repeated.

Benjamin offered the men a cup of coffee, which they accepted. Benjamin noticed that while one of the men was talking the other would be looking about the camp. He gave no indication that he saw what they were doing. They talked on for a while about the journey and the men departed

Salina was very apprehensive. Carrie and Lillie stayed close to her. Beth stayed in their wagon with baby Michael. Mr. Mercer and Jamie stayed in the shadow of their wagons with their guns ready. Abigail and Emily were so frightened they stayed in their wagon. The strangers finally left unsure of just how many people were in the wagon train. That night they doubled the guard. John and Jamie took the eight-o-clock to midnight watch. Mr. Mercer and Charlie took the midnight to four A.M. shift and Will and Aaron took the late watch. They all kept the campfire burning bright and their rifles ready. The men did not return and the Sunday activities went on as usual.

Monday morning as they broke camp King was nowhere to be seen. John and Charlie and the girls searched everywhere for him but to no avail. Jamie and Emily came over to help in the search. After delaying the start of the journey for three hours to search for the dog, Mr. Mercer and Aaron started on. They had agreed to wait on the eastern edge of Poplar Bluff.

They would shop for supplies and wait for the Street's to catch up. At noon they still had not found a trace of King. Ben decided they must start on. They forded the St. Francis River. John and Charlie went to the campsite where they had seen the gypsy's campfire. The gypsies had moved out sometime during the night. There were no dog paw prints to be seen. It was with heavy hearts the Street family continued their journey. King had been a part of their family for many years. It would not be the same without him, especially for John.

It was the next day before they met with the rest of the wagon train as planned. They traveled at a steady pace until nearly six o-clock that evening.

On Thursday morning as John awoke and climbed out of the wagon, King was lying by the rear of the wagon. He had a rope around his neck that he had chewed through to escape. He had whip marks on his back, which were so deep they were oozing blood. His paws were so sore and had cuts on them. He was so thin and looked as if he had not been fed for the three days he had been gone. John picked him up and gently laid him in the back of his wagon. He woke the rest of the family and everyone gathered around. Salina sent Charlie to put logs on the fire and heat some water. Carrie and Lillie went to get her medical bag from the wagon. When the water was heated Salina gently bathed the wounds and applied ointments to King's back and feet and clean bandages around his paws. Charlie brought him some bacon and bread but he was too weak to eat. He just laid his head on John's leg and went to sleep.

After they had eaten breakfast and broke camp, King woke up and whimpered. John stopped his wagon and carried King to the front of his wagon near his seat and laid him on an old quilt. He placed food and water near King and started his wagon again. Some time that afternoon King was able to eat and drink a little and by the next day he was much better.

Everyone believed the gypsies had stolen King because John had refused to sell him. They continued to double the guard and keep big fires burning at night for fear the gypsies might return or be traveling close by.

Since leaving Poplar Bluff they had been traveling thorough rolling hills but now they were getting steeper and the road rougher. They were getting close to the Arkansas border.

Friday night of the sixth week they were camped near a large spring at a town on the Arkansas-Missouri border known as Mammoth Spring. They had never seen such a large spring. The river started from the spring and the water was so cold and clear they filled cups and drank from it. They decided to camp there for the weekend and talk to the local people about property available around the area.

Benjamin went into the general store and talked with people who gave him information about property in Sharp County, which could be homesteaded.

The people were friendly. Family and community seemed to be important to them. Benjamin liked their attitude and felt they had made a wise decision in moving to Arkansas.

On Monday they broke camp early hoping to reach Hardy, the county seat of Sharp County by that evening.

The hills were the steepest they had encountered thus far and the traveling was much slower than they had expected.

On Tuesday evening they reached the town of Hardy and camped on the south edge of town along the banks of Spring River. This was the same river that began at the large spring on the Arkansas-Missouri border where they had camped just two days ago.

That night everyone gathered around the campfire. There was sense of accomplishment, sadness and excitement. They were thankful to have made the trip safely yet sad that they soon would be going their separate ways. Everyone wondered where there would be land to homestead. Would they live near one another? It was a time of relaxation and fellowship. Perhaps the last they would share with people who had became as close as family.

On Wednesday morning the men folk went into town to the courthouse and land office. There they talked with an agent to find where they could homestead land.

"There is a lot of land in the area just north of the town of Williford. It is hilly but it would be good for orchards and livestock. There is also a small amount of land south west of here near the Strawberry River. Let's look on the map and I can show you just where it is located."

Benjamin, Will and John each chose eighty acres in the area north of Williford.

Mr. Mercer chose eighty acres a little farther north that had a log cabin someone had built several years before and then abandoned.

Aaron McKay chose eighty acres near the Strawberry River. After signing the papers and thanking the agent they returned to camp. Everyone was excited to hear where his or her new homes would be.

As Aaron and Beth said good-by to the Streets, Beth hugged Salina and said, "I'll never forget you. You have taught me so much about life and how to care for my family. Please come and visit us when we get our home built."

Benjamin and Salina promised they would visit when they had a chance. Carrie and Lillie hugged baby Michael. They would miss him.

Aaron and Beth turned their wagon south and crossed the Spring River on the old wooden swinging bridge. Their land was located along the Strawberry River just east of the town of Evening Shade. They still had a day's journey to reach it. It seemed strange to them to be traveling alone.

The Streets and the Mercers headed southeast. They reached a steep, very high hill just before sundown. They decided to camp for the night and scout the best route over the hill in the morning.

The next morning Ben and Charlie rode horses up the hill and returned to report it would take two teams to pull each wagon up the hill it was so steep and rough. They hooked the Mercer's two teams of horses to one on his wagons. Mr. Mercer took the reins and Jamie rode one of the Street's horses. He and Charlie hooked ropes to the tongue of the wagon to help pull the wagon up the hill. Benjamin took the reins on his wagon. John and Will rode the other horses. They hooked their ropes to Ben's wagon to pull it wagon up the hill. Progress was slow. Carrie, Lillie and Emily walked beside the wagons, while Salina and Abigail waited at the bottom of the hill with the other wagons.

The girls waited at the top of the hill while the men returned for the other wagons. It was afternoon before they had all the wagons at the top of the hill. Shortly after they had reached the top of the hill the Mercer family turned north toward their land. They stopped to say good-by. Salina and Abigail promised to visit. Benjamin and Mr. Mercer shook hands and offered help if either of them ever needed it. Jamie shook hands with John and said he would come over and visit with him and King sometime soon. Emily and Lillie had tears in their eyes as they said good-by and hugged each other.

They promised to be friends when they started school. Carrie came out of the wagon carrying the kitten, Speckles and handed him to Emily. Emily looked at her mother and father with a question on her face.

Mrs. Mercer spoke, “Yes, you may have the kitten Emily.”

Mr. Mercer did not say a word. Emily buried her face in the kitten’s soft fur and tears of joy fell. She would never forget her first true friends and the wonderful gift they had given her. She climbed onto the wagon still holding the kitten and each family went their separate ways.

A short distance from the top of the hill the Streets turned down a dirt trail through forests of huge oak and hickory trees. When they reached an open field. Benjamin took out the map the land agent had given him and found the boundaries of his land.

“I believe this is where our land starts. See, here is the field the land agent described. Farther down in the valley is the creek with a spring.” They started on down the trail and stopped at the crest of the hill. The whole family looked down on a wooded valley ablaze with color. Hugh oak trees were various shades of gold, brown and dark red. Hickory trees were a bright yellow and gold. The hickory and oak trees formed a canopy over the dogwood and redbud trees, with their leaves of brilliant red. The creek and spring flowing through the valley formed the most beautiful scene they had ever seen. Even the boys were in awe of the beauty of the splendid scene they were viewing.

Carrie stood for a long moment taking in the beauty of the valley. Finally she spoke, "Mama, what a beautiful place to call home."

"Yes, Carrie it really is a beautiful place for a home."

ARKANSAS
EIGHT

They moved the wagons down the hillside along a small creek with a spring of clear cool water flowing from rocks in the hillside. There they made camp for the night. As Salina cooked supper that night over the campfire, she felt a sense of belonging that she had not felt since leaving Indiana. It seemed strange to only have her family in the camp. She wondered what Aaron and Beth and the Mercers were doing.

Before sunset Charlie and John had gone exploring along the creek and up the hillside. Will had settled down to write a letter to Evie. Carrie and Lillie stayed close to camp for they were afraid there might be wild animals lurking about.

John and Charlie returned to report they had seen smoke from a cabin in the distance so they must have neighbors close by.

John took the first watch that night. The family felt a little vulnerable without the other families they had traveled with for so many weeks.

After breakfast the next morning, Benjamin, Will and John walked through the woods to inspect the land that they had homesteaded. Benjamin felt a sense of security in knowing he owned land again. He took a can of red paint with which he marked trees around the boundary of their property. He also marked and X on trees that were about ten inches in diameter and straight enough to be used to build a cabin. They returned to the campsite at noon. After noon

Will, Benjamin and Charlie went into the small town of Williford to purchase supplies they were in need of.

At the general store, Ben asked where he could purchase windows and other hardware he would need for the cabin. The proprietor of the store said he could order what they needed from Jonesboro. Ben was pleased to hear this information.

Will asked where the post office was located and was given directions. After mailing his letters to Evie, he walked around the town. The depot seemed to be very busy with people waiting to board the train. There was a little white church next to a small cemetery located farther up the hill. Also, there were several general stores, a hotel and a small jail. The town was smaller than Princeton. But it was larger than some they had passed through on their way to Arkansas.

Will returned to the general store where he had left his father. Ben was talking to several men. One was a burley man with thick dark hair. As Will approached the group, Ben introduced Will to the man whose name was Polk Crabtree.

"Mr. Crabtree lives near us." Ben said.

"My cabin is just over the hill from your camp. I saw the light from your campfire last night. I wondered if someone had homesteaded the land or was just passing through."

"We have come from near Princeton, Indiana." Ben said. We are homesteading the land from the creek up past the open field."

A man sitting near a potbellied stove in the rear of the store muttered just loud enough for Benjamin to hear, "Yankees. More damn Yankees."

Benjamin heard him and knew he was being judged and his future standing in the town would depend on his action this very minute. Benjamin walked to where the man was sitting, extended his hand and said, "My name is Benjamin Street. What is your name?"

The man mumbled his name was Jones but refused to accept the hand Benjamin offered.

"There are no Yankees or Rebels anymore. The war has been over for a long time and I prefer to keep it that way." Ben turned and walked back to where Will, Charlie and Polk Crabtree were standing. Polk reached out to shake his hand and Benjamin knew he had made a friend. The storekeeper who had watched in silence now was all smiles. He began to write up Ben's order for the windows and hardware he needed. "Will that be all for you?" he asked.

"I will need a cast iron cook stove later on but I will order it closer to the time when I need it."

Polk Crabtree was ready to leave for home at the same time as Ben. They traveled together. Polk stopped by the camp and was introduced to the rest of the family.

"Do you know anyone who makes shingles?" Benjamin asked.

"I made the ones for my cabin. If you want, you can come over tomorrow and look at the ones I made. I will come over and help raise your cabin if you need me."

"I will take you up on that offer but only if you will allow me to return the favor sometime." Ben promised to come over tomorrow for the families to get aquatinted.

NINE

After they returned home there was still two hours of daylight left. The men walked through the woods and continued marking the trees they would cut to build their cabin.

Salina and the girls began preparation for the evening meal. There was a chill in the late afternoon air. Salina longed for the comfort of four walls and a roof around her. She knew soon she would have a proper home. Benjamin had promised her. She knew he would keep his word.

That night they unloaded some of the things from the wagons and Charlie and Will slept in the wagon with John. Just after dark a fine mist of rain began to fall and a damp chill settled over the camp. The wind was blowing briskly so they were not able to keep a fire going. No one slept much that night. When daybreak came Will rose first and built a roaring fire. After breakfast they made ready to visit their new neighbors. Salina might not have a home yet, but she would be dressed properly when she went calling on her neighbors for the first time. John decided to stay behind to watch the camp. Charlie offered to stay with him but John refused his offer. The family climbed into the smallest of the wagons and traveled the short distance to Polk Crabtree's homestead.

They pulled the wagon up in front of a large log cabin with huge oak trees in front. Polk and his wife came out of the cabin to greet them. Mrs. Crabtree was delighted to have neighbors so close. She welcomed them warmly and invited them into the cabin.

Polk, Ben, Will and Charlie went around the house to inspect the shingles Polk had made. He showed Ben how he made them from white oak logs.

"White oak seems to stand the weather better and doesn't seem to crack as bad." Polk said. "I'd be happy to come over and lend a hand when your are ready.

"We'll be grateful for any help and we'll repay you if and when you need help." Ben answered.

The men went into the cabin where Mrs. Crabtree was serving coffee and homemade blackberry cobbler with thick cream over it. Just as the men sat down at the table, the Crabtree's daughter Laura came out of the kitchen.

Charlie looked up to see the most beautiful girl he had ever seen. In that instant he lost his heart to the girl he would love all his life.

Laura had long thick dark brown hair and blue eyes, her high cheekbones and finely chiseled features were set in skin as smooth and creamy as ivory. At the age of fifteen, even with the loose fitting cotton dress she wore, you could see her figure was beginning to blossom into young womanhood.

Charlie could do nothing but stare at her. When Ben introduced the family to Laura, Charlie could only mumble a greeting.

Laura was very conscious of Charlie staring at her and felt very ill at ease with him. They finished eating and the Street family prepared to leave. The Crabtree family went with them and took a wagon loaded with tools and saws. When they arrived they found John sharpening the axes and saws and preparing to start cutting the trees for their cabin.

Benjamin found a level place along the creek to build the cabin. For the next two weeks they sawed down trees with a crosscut saw and trimmed them into logs for the cabin. They hooked chains around the logs and used the horses to pull them to where they were to build the cabin. On Saturday morning Ben and the boys went into town for supplies and to check on the windows and hardware he had ordered.

As they were loading the wagon, Polk came by and inquired how they were doing with building of the cabin.

"We think we have enough logs cut and trimmed for the cabin. We plan to start building on Monday. We are stopping by the sawmill on the way home to pick up the lumber for the floor."

"I'll be over to help raise the walls. That can be a hard job if you don't have enough help."

"Bring Mrs. Crabtree and the family with you. Salina will make dinner for everyone and the women can get better acquainted."

"I'll do that." Polk answered. He waved good-by and started toward home.

It was the beginning of the second week of November and the weather was getting cooler each day and the nights were cold. There had been frost a few mornings when John had rose to rekindle the fire. The daylight hours were getting shorter and Benjamin knew he had only a short time to get the cabin built. He knew what a hardship the winter would be for Salina. He had risen earlier than usual that morning and he and his sons were already placing the logs for the foundation when the Crabtree's arrived.

Ben had leveled two sides of several large logs to form the foundation. Next they laid a floor from the lumber they had bought at the sawmill. This was done by noon and in the afternoon they got two rows of logs up on walls. Ben got the bags of cement from the wagon and Charlie, Lillie and Carrie carried sand and water from the creek and mixed mortar to seal between the logs. Even Laura helped with the last load of sand and water.

Laura had become more comfortable around Charlie as the day had worn on and Charlie was no longer tongue tied around her. In fact they teased each other and laughed a lot. Now Charlie understood why Will had been so reluctant to leave Indiana and why he wrote a letter to Evie each night.

The weather stayed warm for a few more days and by the end of the week the walls were up and the cracks between the logs were sealed. On Saturday morning Benjamin and Will went to the sawmill for more lumber for the roof. Charlie and John stayed at home and continued to work on the cabin. Polk came over and began making shingles for the roof. Charlie and John watched and with a few lessons from Polk were making shingles by the time Ben and Will returned.

Will and Charlie climbed the scaffold and Ben and John passed the boards up to them. Soon the roof decking was completed and they began placing the shingles. This took longer and they did not accomplish much before nightfall.

Early Monday morning they began laying shingles again and by Wednesday the roof was finished. Benjamin began building the fireplace with stones they had carried from the creek. By late Friday afternoon the cabin was completed. There were only two small rooms but Benjamin had promised Salina a bigger house soon.

The family slept in the wagons that night for the last time. On Saturday morning they began moving into the cabin. With the extra lumber Benjamin was building bed frames along the walls to hold the mattress and feather beds they had brought with them. Next he built a trestle table with benches along each side and chairs for he and Salina.

The cabin had seemed large enough before they began moving their belongings in. Now it seemed crowded and small. Salina cooked supper that night over the large open fireplace. The fire warmed the cabin and it felt so cozy. The family slept that night underneath their own roof for the first time since leaving Indiana. Will thought of Evie and the cabin he would build for her. Charlie dreamed of Laura and wondered what life held for them. Carrie and Lillie talked of Emily and wondered if she felt as cozy and safe in her new home as they felt in theirs.

John was restless. He had seen the flashes of light again today while he was caring for the animals. He had lain down on the ground for a while. No seizure had followed but his head had hurt most of the day. He had said nothing about this to mama or dad.

Benjamin and Salina talked for a while. Benjamin promised to build them a bigger house as soon as he could.

The following Thursday was Thanksgiving. Benjamin and Salina invited the Crabtree family to dinner. Salina prepared a meal of baked ham, German potato salad, homemade cottage cheese and dried peach and apple pies. Mrs. Crabtree brought vegetables and Blackberry cobbler. The day was spent visiting, playing music and singing.

Benjamin and Salina were thankful to have made the journey from Indiana safely and to have made such good friends as the Crabtree family.

The next few weeks were spent settling into the cabin, cutting firewood and logs to build a corral for the livestock. Every one in the family seemed happy and content except for Will. He missed Evie terribly. He wrote letters to her every night and mailed them every Saturday. Charlie knew how much Will missed Evie. He would find every chance he could to visit the Crabtree cabin to see Laura.

Christmas came and Benjamin and Will cut a beautiful Cedar tree for a Christmas tree. Carrie and Lillie decorated it.

"It really feels like home." Lillie said as they finished the tree.

"I still miss Mary, Lottie, Mag and Nellie." Carrie said. "If they were here it would be perfect."

Indiana now seemed a long way away, as if that was another world. Christmas day was a joyous time with presents for the children and Salina prepared a delicious Christmas dinner.

That afternoon Charlie walked over to see Laura. Benjamin had given him some money. He had bought Laura a silk scarf for Christmas. They walked down by the creek and Charlie gave Laura the gift. She loved the scarf and tied it around her neck. They walked and talked until the sun began to set.

There was a chill in the air as Charlie walked Laura home and it was dark by the time he got home.

When he arrived home he found the family gathered around John as he lay on the floor. He was having another seizure. When the seizure activity subsided they lifted him onto the bed and undressed him. He slept until morning. This was the first seizure her had since leaving Indiana.

The second week of February the weather turned bitterly cold. The temperatures dropped to below zero at night. But the family was warm and cozy in their little cabin. Then two weeks later the yellow daffodils were blooming and the trees were beginning to bud.

In early March Benjamin and the boys planted the apple and peach trees they had brought from Indiana. On warm days during the winter they had cleared a large tract of land farther up on the hillside for an orchard. Benjamin had decided it would be a good place to build a larger house one day. In the large field at the top of the hill they planted a large garden and cornfield. There was good grass on part of the field for hay. As the spring turned to summer the crops thrived and the family looked forward to a bountiful harvest. The young fruit trees should bare a good crop of fruit in a few years.

One evening a few weeks later as the family was eating the evening meal Benjamin said, "I think we need a larger house, one with an upstairs, with a bedroom for the girls and one for the boys. I thought when the corn crop was gathered we could start cutting the logs. We should have it done before winter. Then when Will and Evie are married they could live in this little cabin until they can build a bigger home."

"Dad, I don't want to stay in Arkansas." Will said. "I have made up my mind to go back to Indiana. I think Evie and I will be happier living there. I will have a better chance to find work there. I don't think I want to farm but I don't know what I really want to do right now. But I know I don't want to stay here.

Salina was shocked. She had counted on Will to be near them when he and Evie were married. Now all her married children would be so far away. With an ache in her heart she waited as Benjamin spoke.

"When did you decide this, son?"

"I have been thinking about it for a long time but just decided today. I'll stay and help you get the bigger cabin built before I leave, but I would like to be back in Indiana before December."

"I appreciate the offer to stay while we build the new cabin. We will need your help and with good weather the house should be finished by December."

It was the last week of August, just a year since they had left Indiana. But to Carrie it seemed a lifetime ago. And now Will had told them he would be going back soon. Her family seemed to be getting smaller all the time.

Benjamin and Salina Street
Carrie Street Beavers
Dorothy and Howard Beavers

TEN

The new cabin was nearly completed by mid November. When Benjamin returned from town on Saturday he had a cast iron cook stove with him. Salina was thrilled. For over a year she had been cooking on campfires and the big fireplace. She had missed the huge old stove she had left behind. The new one was smaller but it had a warming closet on top and a water reservoir so she would have warm water available. Benjamin and the boys moved the stove into the new cabin. Benjamin built a chimney for it. By the end of the next week they were moved into the new house. There was a bedroom upstairs for Carrie and Lillie and across the hall one for the boys. Benjamin and Salina would sleep downstairs. Benjamin had made bed frames that were not attached to the walls. He made headboards and footboards of oak and hickory.

He also made Deacon's benches to place in front of the fireplace. Salina took cotton batting and some of her print fabric and sewed cushions for the benches. The new cabin began to look more like a permanent home.

The week after they were settled in their new home Will decided it was time for him to leave for Indiana. He and John walked through the woods where the brightly colored leaves had fallen in deep piles. Some were still clinging to the trees even though it was the beginning of December. The weather was still warm during the day. Will and John talked for hours.

"If you ever want to come back to Indiana you can stay with Evie and me." Will said.

"I miss my friends in Indiana." John said. "Especially Lizzie and Pearl Mahan and Perry Thomas. Perhaps I'll come for a visit after you and Evie are married. I'll write and I will expect you to let me know about everyone there."

On the first Saturday in December the family went with Will to the train station. Salina's heart was breaking yet she was happy to know that Will and Evie would soon be married. She had been present when her two oldest daughters were married. But she would not be there to see the first of her sons married.

As they waited at the train depot, Benjamin handed Will an envelope containing money. Will protested that he did not want to take the money but Benjamin insisted.

"You have postponed you plans for a year and a half. Your mother and I want you to have this to help you and Evie get started. We feel we owe you this much."

Will protested again. "You don't owe me anything dad. I will miss you and mama and the family. But I just don't feel that Arkansas is the place for Evie and me."

With tears in her eyes Salina spoke. "You have given so much to your family we want you to have a happy life with Evie."

A whistle signaled the train's arrival at the station. There were hugs and good-byes. Will promised to write soon and to let them know all of the wedding plans. He boarded the train, waved his hand and disappeared into the train. The whistle blew to signal the train's departure and Will was gone. With a feeling of emptiness the family climbed into the wagon and started home.

ELEVEN

Two weeks later there was a letter from Will telling of his safe arrival in Indiana. There was news of his sister's and their families and plans for his and Evie's wedding. They would be married in September of the following year. Will wanted to wait until he could find work and save enough money to have a proper home for Evie.

When Christmas was near Carrie and Lillie decorated the tree John and Charlie cut down. On Christmas Eve the Street and Crabtree families gathered at the Street's cabin to celebrate. Charlie had walked over with Laura. Laura's family had been there for a while when Laura and Charlie arrived. As they toasted the Holiday Season Charlie made the announcement.

"Mr. and Mrs. Crabtree, Laura and I would like to get married."

The announcement shocked both families. Benjamin and Salina did not know what to say.

Mr. and Mrs. Crabtree did not say anything for a few minutes but anger showed on their faces.

Benjamin was the first to speak. "You are both only sixteen. Charlie how will you earn a living? Where will you live?

"Dad, I love Laura. I will get a job at the sawmill. We could live in our first cabin down by the creek. Mr. Crabtree, I will take good care of Laura."

Finally Mrs. Crabtree spoke. "Laura you are both so young. You have lots of time to get married."

For the rest of the evening conversation centered around trying to persuade the young couple that they were to young to handle the responsibilities of marriage. But Charlie and Laura remained steadfast in their determination to be married. Finally the young couple agreed to wait until they were seventeen. Charlie would be seventeen on April 28th.

Laura's birthday was September 25th. Charlie and Laura decided they would be married in October just after Laura's birthday.

Relationships between the two families were strained as the Crabtree's said good-by and left for home.

Charlie walked Laura home and returned after the family had gone to bed. He climbed the stairs to the room he shared with John. He found him still awake reading by the oil lamp.

"John do you think I am wrong to want to marry Laura?"

"I don't think you are wrong if you really love her. I do think you are awfully young for the responsibilities of a wife and family." John replied.

"I know we are very young, but I want to have as much time with Laura as I can. Even if we are married as long as mama and dad it won't be long enough. I really love her. I know it won't be easy, but being with Laura will be worth it."

"Then if you feel that strongly about Laura, then marry her." John said. "But remember marriage is a lifetime commitment and a great responsibility."

As they blew out the lamp and tried to sleep their minds were a mixture of emotions. John was sure Charlie believed he loved Laura, but he wondered if they had any idea of what responsibilities they would face. He also wondered why he had never found someone he felt as strongly about as Will did Evie and now as Charlie felt about Laura. He had always felt his life had been predestined for him and he was not meant to make a commitment to any one.

Charlie thought of Laura and living in the small cabin and having a family. He had kissed for the first time tonight and his lips still felt the warm glow from the touch of hers.

As New Years Eve came that year there was great excitement, for this was not only the beginning of a new year and a new decade, but also the start of a new century. The family saw the new century begin together. At midnight the sound of gunfire and bells could be heard throughout the hills and valleys. Benjamin, John and Charlie went into the yard and fired their guns. Lillie and Carrie rang the dinner bell.

Spring came early that year. The redbud and dogwood trees were a mass of blooms. The yellow bell and fire bushes Salina had planted that first spring were in full bloom. Salina and Carrie thought this was the most beautiful place they had ever seen.

TWELVE

As the summer came Laura and Charlie were busy making plans to be married. Charlie had found work and also began work on a cabin where they would live. He and Laura had decided they wanted their own cabin and found a level spot of land just across the valley from the Street cabin and a short distance from the Crabtree homestead.

Laura and Charlie were married October 14, 1900 and set up housekeeping in their small cabin and soon Laura was expecting a child. Charlie felt life could never be any better.

Salina felt her house was getting so empty. But she saw Charlie and Laura often. And the news that they expected a baby thrilled her. She kept busy with John, Carrie and Lillie.

Thanksgiving and Christmas came and went and they settled into a routine for the winter. John was looking thinner and had become quieter. He spent a lot of time walking in the woods with King at his side. Salina worried about him but when she questioned him about it, he said he was fine and enjoyed being by himself in the woods.

In the spring of 1901 Salina received word that Mary had married Floyd Caniff on March 21st. Salina felt more homesick for her family in Indiana than she had since leaving.

In June, word came that Lottie and Ollie Belcher had been married on June 6th. Salina again felt the pangs of homesickness but she hid it from Benjamin, and the children.

That summer they had some of the hottest weather Salina and Benjamin had ever felt. Temperatures were over 100 degrees during the day and only dropped into the 80's at night.

On July 16th, Laura gave birth to a son they named Perry. Charlie felt he would burst with pride. Salina and Mrs. Crabtree took turns caring for the baby and Laura. Salina had missed being with her daughters and grandchildren and was happy to have a baby in the family again.

As July passed into August the hot temperatures continued to scorch the hills. Trees began to turn brown and crops failed. Cattle and livestock were dying for lack of water. Benjamin, John, Carrie and Lillie carried water from the spring to keep their cattle alive.

One hot afternoon as Benjamin and Salina rested, Carrie and Lillie walked down to the creek, took off their shoes, lifted their skirts and waded in the cool water. As they returned home they stopped by the barn with fresh water they had brought for the kittens. They found John on the barn floor having a seizure.

Carrie screamed, "Lillie, run to the house and get mama and dad!!" Carrie tried to hold John as his body writhed and jerked with the seizure. Benjamin and Salina arrived just as the jerking motions ceased and John's body stiffened and then began to relax. Carrie and Lillie helped Benjamin carry John's still form to the house where they placed him on the bed in the bedroom downstairs. After several hours John showed no response and was not awakening from the seizure. Salina sent Benjamin to town to fetch the doctor.

When they arrived, the doctor examined John and found no signs of response, even when he pricked his skin with a pin.

"I am afraid your son will not recover from this seizure. He is in a deep coma and will only sink deeper into one within the next few days."

A fear such as Salina had never known gripped her heart. "Are you saying John will not get over this seizure?"

"I don't see any way John can come out of this coma. He is in a very deep state of unconsciousness now and I believe it will only worsen with time. I wish there were more encouraging news, but I want to be honest with you. I don't believe John will get any better."

Salina's heart was heavy as she sank into a chair by John's bed. Benjamin paid the doctor and thanked him for coming. His heart was breaking at the thought of losing his eldest son. He had thought John would be here to take care of Salina and the girls when he was gone. Now the doctor had said John would be gone before him. How could he bear this pain of losing his eldest son?

Benjamin had seen many young men killed and maimed in the Civil War. He had felt pain and sadness at their death, but that was nothing to compare with what he was feeling now. He did not know what to do. He went into the barn and began oiling the tools and cleaning and oiling the saddles and tack just as John had always done.

Carrie went into the room where Salina was sitting by John. She sat down on the bed next to John and held his hand. Throughout the night Salina and Carrie bathed John's face and hands with cool water from the spring.

Word had spread throughout the valley that there was sickness at the Street cabin. Neighbors came and went through out the day, bringing food and words of encouragement and offers to help in any way they could.

Salina and Carrie maintained their vigil at the bedside, aware that people were coming and going but no one intruded on their sorrow. Benjamin and Charlie talked with the people who came by. Laura had taken baby Perry and gone to stay with her mother so Charlie could be there for his family.

The dawn came and there was no improvement in John's condition. Benjamin carried food into Salina and Carrie but neither of them was able to eat.

Lillie had gone to bed but had not slept at all. She had never known anyone close to her who had died. She wondered what John was feeling. Was he in pain? Did he know he was dying? Was he afraid? There were no answers for her. She had always gone to Carrie with questions she did not understand. Now Carrie was with her mother and John.

As the sun rose higher John lingered, hovering between life and death. Salina and Carrie alternated between feelings or hope and despair. If only John could get better!!

A few minutes after the clock had struck ten-o-clock, Carrie watched as John's breathing slowed and became shallow. She looked up to meet Salina's eyes and they both knew John's life was about to end. A long, last breath escaped from John's lips. Carrie watched as the pulse in John's neck slowly stopped beating. She looked into her mother's eyes and saw a pain more intense than she had ever seen before. Carrie felt crushing pain in her own chest and felt she would not be able to breath.

Finally Salina was able to speak. "Carrie, go tell your father to come to me. Our son is dead." Salina spoke the words haltingly, as if they did not want to come from her lips. She placed her hand over John's face and slowly closed his eyes. This child she had given birth to was now dead and a part of her was gone forever.

Carrie stumbled from the room and found her father in the yard with Charlie and several men from the neighborhood.

"Dad, mama said to come to her." was all Carrie could say. Tears streamed down her cheeks. "Where is Lillie?" she asked.

"She walked down toward the spring." Charlie spoke the words with a lump in throat and pain in his heart.

No one asked any questions. Every one sensed that death had come to the Street cabin.

Benjamin slowly walked into the cabin where he found Salina standing by the bed where John lay so still and pale. He walked to Salina and placed a hand on her shoulder.

"I will go to town and send telegrams to Will and the girls in Indiana. Then I will stop by the sawmill and get lumber to build a coffin for John.

"Get white satin and cotton batting for me to line it with." Salina spoke the words but they seem to come from someone else's lips. She could not believe she and Benjamin were standing by the body of their son, calmly discussing his coffin. She wanted to scream and beat her fists against the wall. But instead she stood there calmly telling Ben what she would need from the store.

"I'll bathe and dress John while you are gone and you can shave him when you return."

"You need to rest while I am gone I will help you when I get back home. You haven't slept all night." Benjamin said.

"Where is Carrie? She stayed with me throughout this whole ordeal?"

"She went to look for Lillie. She had walked down toward the creek. I suppose she went to the Crabtree's to be with Laura and the baby." Benjamin replied.

"I think I will rest for awhile and then take care of John." Salina said. She slowly climbed the stairs to the girl's room and lay down on the bed. Tears slid down her cheeks and her body shook with silent sobs. Finally she fell into an exhausted sleep.

"I must go to town and send telegrams to Will and the girls and get supplies to build John's coffin. Charlie will you go with me?"

"Charlie you go with your dad." Polk said, "I will go tell Laura and take care of her and the baby."

Charlie wanted to be with Laura and to hold his baby son, but knew his dad needed him now so he hitched the team. It seemed an eternity since they had found John slumped on the hay in the barn. Everywhere they looked in the barn there were signs of John, where he had lovingly cared for the animals and tools.

Neither of them spoke on the long ride into town. Their thoughts were some where in the past when a gentle son and brother had been so much a part of their lives and was no more.

Carrie walked toward the spring. She knew where Lillie could be found. The first year they had lived in Arkansas, she and Lillie had discovered a large flat rock along the creek bank. It was sheltered on three sides by bushes. They had claimed this spot as their secret place and had spent many hours there telling secrets and wondering about their future. Who would they marry? Where would they live? Would they live close to one another?

Now Carrie found Lillie in their secret place. She was sitting with her arms locked around her knees and her face pressed against her legs. Great sobs shook her body. Carrie sat down by her little sister and placed her arm around her shoulders.

"Oh! Carrie what will we do without John?" She cried. "All our family is leaving us. What will we do if mama and dad die?"

"Mama and dad won't die for a long time and we will always have each other." Carrie said as tears streamed down her face. She did not feel reassured but was trying to comfort Lillie and share her grief. The girls sat for a long time talking and sharing the sorrow of John's death.

Finally Carrie said, "We must go, mama may need us." They returned to the cabin and found Salina in the bedroom with John. She had bathed him and dressed him. Now he looked as if he were only asleep. The girls looked into the room but could not bring themselves to go in. They busied themselves in the kitchen. Lillie sliced the homemade bread and made tea while Carrie cooked meat and vegetables from the garden.

Benjamin sent the telegrams to the family in Indiana and bought the supplies Salina needed. They stopped by the sawmill on the way home and Ben bought pine lumber for John's coffin.

When they returned home Charlie went the Crabtree's cabin. He needed to be with Laura and baby Perry. He could not imagine what it would be like to lose his baby son.

Polk came over and he and Ben soon had a coffin built for John. They carried it to the front room of the cabin and placed it on Ben's sawhorses. Salina came from John's room and began lining the coffin with cotton batting and the white satin. While she did this, Ben went to the bedroom and shaved John's still face. Polk and Ben carried the coffin into the room where John's body lay and placed it in the coffin. Ben folded John's hands together and then he and Polk carried the coffin back to the front room.

King, who rarely came into the house, crept in and lay at the foot of John's coffin all night. Some time just before daybreak he slipped out of the house and was never seen again.

It was late afternoon now and people throughout the hills had heard that the quiet, gentle John Street had passed away. People came and went throughout the evening and into the night. Some brought food. Carrie and Lillie busied themselves making coffee and tea. Benjamin and Salina kept a vigil by their son's coffin.

Sometime after midnight Carrie and Lillie went upstairs and lay down. Both were sure they would not sleep. But finally exhaustion took over and they fell into a sleep filled with dreams of Indiana and the family they had left behind. Carrie dreamed she was running through the fields of the farm in Indiana looking for her father, but she could not find him. Then she came upon the body of a young man who looked like John. He was lying face down. But when she turned him over it was her father. She awoke with her body shaking and tears running down her face. She never told anyone of the dream, not even Lillie.

As daylight came the temperature was already rising toward 90 degrees. But Salina and Ben dressed in their black Sunday clothes.

Around ten-o-clock Charlie and Polk arrived to help load John's coffin into the wagon. Ben and Salina rode in the wagon with John. Carrie and Lillie rode in the wagon with Charlie and Laura. They made their way to the Baker Cemetery. Along the way friends and neighbors joined the funeral procession. Several men of the community had dug John's grave along side the fence under a large tree.

The temperature was now over 100 degrees and Salina was not sure she would be able to stand the heat much longer.

The minister read the funeral service and the congregation sang hymns. When the service was over several men placed ropes under John's coffin and slowly lowered it into the grave. Salina felt as if her chest would explode with the pain she was feeling. The unbearable heat was making her dizzy.

Carrie and Lillie led her away from the crowd. They wet Benjamin's handkerchief with water someone had brought and bathed her face. Soon she felt some better.

Abigail Mercer and Emily came over to where they were standing. Abigail hugged Salina and Emily hugged Carrie and Lillie. They sat for a while talking of the journey they had made from Indiana.

Abigail told Salina they were going back to Indiana. James had not prospered as he had thought they would and was becoming restless. Emily and Jamie did not want to return. All three of them knew things would be no different in Indiana.

Jamie came over and reached out his hand to hold Salina's. "Mrs. Street, John was my first and best friend. I shall never forget him. He taught me so much about life. I know if I ever amount to anything in my life it will be because he was my friend."

Salina held Jamie's hand. "John would be proud to know you thought of him in that way. I am sure he knew you were his friend."

Jamie left his mother and Mrs. Street, walked down the hill to a small creek, sat down on a log, buried his face in his hands and wept.

The friends and neighbors were beginning to leave. Benjamin and Salina found the girls. They walked by the open grave and looked for the last time at the coffin holding John's body. They turned away, went to the wagon and left for home. Neighborhood men began filling the grave.

When the family returned home, Salina went into the bedroom removed her Sunday dress and lay down on the bed. Ben cared for the horses. Carrie and Lillie changed their clothes and walked down to their secret place near the spring. They drank cool water from the spring and cooled their feet in the creek below the spring. They talked for hours. The sun was setting when they returned to the cabin.

They found Salina in the kitchen preparing supper. It felt good to be busy in her familiar kitchen. Salina's lips smiled at her daughters but the light was gone from her eyes.

After supper Carrie went to the barn with food for King and the cats. But King was nowhere to be found. They searched until dark but there was no sign of him anywhere. There was no response when they called his name. Finally as dark descended they had to return home.

The next day Charlie told Laura that he had something to do. He saddled his horse and started for the Baker Cemetery. He stopped along the creek and found two large flat stones and placed them in a bag he had slung over the saddle. When he reached the cemetery he sat for a long time thinking of all the things he and John had shared. Things they had talked about while they had done their chores or walked together through the woods. As he sat thinking of the past, he scratched John's name, birth and death dates on the larger of the stones. He placed this stone at the head of John's grave and smaller one at the foot of the grave. The sun was setting when he returned to his little cabin and Laura.

THIRTEEN

Things settled into a routine with Benjamin now taking care of the animals. Sometimes Charlie came over to help with the chores. As August passed into September they began picking the apples. This was the first harvest from the trees they had brought from Indiana.

Word came that Will and Evie had been married on September 5 th.

As the months passed, slowly the light came back into Salina's eyes. Life continued on for the family.

In the fall of 1903 Benjamin and Lillie went to Indiana. Ben needed to file some papers for his Civil War pension. Carrie and Salina stayed at home to care for the animals and the homestead. Also Laura and Charlie were expecting another baby any time. On October 2 nd Laura gave birth to a son they named Willie Ray. Salina loved to care for the grandchildren. She longed to be with her daughters and grandchildren in Indiana.

Benjamin and Lillie returned home with news and pictures of Lottie and Mary's children. The best news was that Mag and her family were moving to Arkansas. Nellie and Tom had also talked of moving somewhere nearby. Salina was thrilled that more of her children were moving closer to her. Carrie was glad to know that her nieces Clara and Mamie would be closer. They had shared many happy times in the years before she had left Indiana. They still wrote letters regularly.

The years passed in a predictable routine. Carrie was approaching twenty years old. She had grown in to a tall, attractive young woman. Several young men of the community were attracted to her. But when any of them paid attention to her, she remembered how uncomfortable she had felt when Jamie Mercer had tried to get her attention as they were traveling to Arkansas. She remained guarded and aloof and preferred to spend time in a group of friends rather than pairing off as a couple with any of the young men her friends introduced her to.

Carrie and Lillie visited with Mag and her family in Mammoth Springs and enjoyed being with a group of young people there. For a short time Carrie worked at a shoe factory there. But she missed her dad and mama and soon returned to the homestead.

Laura gave birth to Bertha January 2, 1906 but the joy was short lived when on February 3rd, Willie died of a fever. He had been sick for only a few days when the frail little body no longer had the strength to breath.

Charlie had felt as if his heart had been ripped from his body when John died but the pain he felt as he laid his little son to rest tore his heart in pieces.

Salina tried to comfort Charlie and Laura but her own grief was mixed with thoughts of her own son and what his loss had meant to her.

As the family prepared to leave another family member buried in the Baker Cemetery, Carrie held tiny little Bertha close. She did not think she could live if she had a child who died. Charlie and Benjamin helped Laura and Salina into the wagons. Carrie handed the baby to Laura and the family left for home.

In the late summer of 1907 Will and Evie and their children came to visit. It was the first time Will had been back since leaving. He liked the way Ben had improved the homestead. The fruit trees they had planted that first spring were now heavy with fruit. Benjamin belonged to a fruit grower's co-op that shipped fruit to St. Louis by train.

Will and Evie's son Glenn was five years old and enjoyed following his grandpa when he did chores. Glen asked questions about everything. Ben took his grandsons to the creek below the house and they played in the water. He picked a watermelon from the patch and the boys helped him haul it to the house. Glen thought he had never tasted watermelon that was so good. Salina and Evie talked for hours. Evie told her of all the news of family and friends back in Indiana. Soon it was time for them to leave. With heavy hearts Benjamin and Salina took them to the train depot.

FOURTEEN

In the spring of 1908 Charlie and some of the other young men of the community cleared a large field on a level spot at the end on Ben's hay field and made a baseball diamond. Every Sunday afternoon groups young men would gather and form teams and play baseball. Soon other teams from Williford and other communities would come to play the Baker community team.

One Sunday in June, the Baker team was playing the team from Williford. Carrie and Lillie were sitting with several other young ladies, when two young men approached. The tall dark headed one was very interested in Lillie and was not shy about letting her know. The other was a stocky built young man with reddish curly hair and a shy manner. He was interested in Carrie, but was not sure how to let her know.

Carrie offered them lemonade from a large jug she had brought from home. Finally Jay Beavers found the courage to ask Carrie her name and where she lived. They talked as they watched the ball game. Jesse Spurgin was telling Lillie that he and Jay had been in Oklahoma working for the railroad.

When the ball game was over Jay asked if he could walk home with Carrie. Jesse and Lillie walked along behind them. Charlie did not know Jay and Jesse so he watched from a distance to be sure his sisters were not in any danger.

Carrie invited the young men in to meet her mama and dad. They came in and sat for a while. Ben told them stories of when he was in the Civil War and of the wagon trip to Arkansas.

Before they left, Jay asked if he could call on Carrie. Benjamin gave his permission but said it was up to Carrie. They made plans to go to the neighborhood dance next Saturday night. Benjamin liked the redheaded young man named Jay. Jesse also asked if he could take Lillie to the dance.

All that summer and into the fall they met every Saturday night and Sunday afternoon. Sometimes they went to dances or just visited with Benjamin and Salina. On Sunday afternoon they usually watched the baseball games. Jay had fallen in love with Carrie that first day he had seen her at the ball field.

In late October Jay got up enough courage to ask Carrie to marry him. Carrie was not sure she wanted to marry anyone. She felt safe and secure living with her mama and dad. She wasn't sure she was ready to leave that security for the unknown. Could she have a marriage like her mother and father's?

Finally one day Carrie told Salina about Jay's proposal. Salina was not surprised. She had seen the way Jay looked at Carrie when they were together.

"Mama, I'm not sure that I want to be married to anyone. I like living here with you and dad and Lillie. I like Jay and we have a lot of fun together but living with someone would be different."

"Carrie, your father and I will not be here forever. All our children except for you and Lillie are settled in their own lives. Your dad and I need to see you and Lillie settled with someone who will care for you. We are both getting on in years. You and Lillie need to be thinking about your future. I am not telling you to marry Jay unless you love him. But if you care enough about him to be his wife don't let fear of the unknown keep you from following you heart."

Mama, don't talk about you and dad dying. I want you to be here for a very long time."

"We want that to Carrie, but that won't be possible. Life is short and we only have an allotted time. It is not how long that life is, but how we spend it that is the measure of our lives. I have hoped to be here to see you and Lillie married. I want to be with you when your babies come. I have missed that with Mary and Lottie."

Jay and Carrie decided they would be married on Christmas Eve. Salina was busy sewing a dress of ivory linen for Carrie's wedding dress.

Jesse and Lillie stood up with Jay and Carrie as they were married by a Justice of the Peace on December 24, 1908. They spent their wedding night in the small two, room house Jay had built for them on the land Carrie had homesteaded when she had come of age.

That night Jay went outside while Carrie got undressed and got into bed. When Jay returned he blew out the oil lamp and got into bed beside Carrie.

Carrie would always find the physical part of love distasteful. But Jay remained and loving and faithful husband for the fifty-three years they were married.

Jay and Carrie settled into their small house just across the valley from Benjamin and Salina. Carrie visited Salina every day.

One day in early April when Carrie was visiting with Salina, they had walked up the hill to the spot where they had stopped that first day to gaze down on the valley that was now their home. Carrie had stopped to pick wild flowers that were growing along the ridge.

"Something is bothering you Carrie. Tell me what it is?"

"I am with child, mama. I am really scared. I have never seen a baby born or never cared for a newborn baby. I helped Laura care for Ruth Ellen when she was born last October but that is all I know about babies. What if I don't know how to care for a child?"

"Everyone is afraid when they have their first baby. But things just come natural and you will learn as the child grows."

Carrie was not completely reassured but felt somewhat better. She and Salina talked until late afternoon. Then Carrie hurried home to make supper for Jay.

Carrie's pregnancy was a happy time for Salina. She sewed tiny garments and made plans to be with Carrie when the baby came.

Salina's joy was marred in June when Lillie announced that she had received a letter from Jesse asking her to come to Bixby, Oklahoma so they could be married. She had written Jesse accepting his proposal.

It was with sadness that Benjamin and Salina took Lillie to the train depot. Salina's heart was as heavy as the day they had brought Will to the depot to return to Indiana.

They hugged Lillie and said their good-bys. Lillie promised to write as soon as she got there. Lillie boarded the train, the whistle blew and Lillie was gone too. Now Benjamin and Salina only had Carrie and Charlie and their families living nearby.

Carrie had not gone to the train depot with Ben and Salina. All alone in her little house she cried as if her heart were broken. She and Lillie had never been separated for more than a days. With the baby coming she had counted on Lillie to be with her.

In Mid July Benjamin came home from town with a letter from Lillie. She and Jesse had been married on July 5 th. Salina was happy for Lillie but missed her terribly.

Charlie and Laura's little girl Bertha became ill and died on August 10 th. Once again the family made the journey to the little cemetery. So much of Salina's heart was buried there. Each time she made the journey she wondered how much longer it would be before she and Benjamin would be buried there.

On September 4, 1909 Carrie and Jay's baby daughter was born. They named her Dorothy. Jay worshipped her from the moment he saw her. A bond was formed that day that would remain unbroken for the rest of their lives.

By 1910 Charlie had developed a persistent cough. Laura and Salina were worried about him. To add to their worries, work had been slow and Charlie had not been able to work very steadily at the sawmill. He decided to leave to look for work elsewhere. His heart was heavy at the thought of leaving Laura, Perry and Ruth. But he knew they needed money to live. His restless nature made him want to try something new.

Charlie boarded a train and went to Corpus Christi, Texas. He found work there and was able to send money back to Laura for her and the children. The warm ocean climate agreed with him and he was soon feeling better and was not coughing as much now. He missed his family terribly and soon returned home.

The years were passing so quickly. On July 8, 1912 Carrie gave birth to a son they named Howard. Carrie took the children to visit with Benjamin and Salina every day. Howard and Dorothy loved to hear the stories Benjamin told and on baking days they always knew their grandma would have baked something special for them. They loved the homemade bread and butter with glasses of cold milk.

Letters came from Lillie with all the news of her life with Jesse and her children.

Laura gave birth to another son on October 5, 1912. Laura and Carrie would meet at Benjamin and Salina's for Dorothy and Ruth to play together.

By 1913 once again work became slow for Charlie and his restless nature began to surface. He had always wanted to go farther west. This time he boarded a train for Denver, Colorado. He arrived there about 11:00 P.M.

Denver was a growing cattle town unlike any Charlie had ever seen. He asked the porter at the depot where he could find a hotel. The porter gave him directions to a modest hotel located near the main section of town. Charlie began walking in the direction he had been given and soon found the hotel. It was clean but the building and furnishings were shabby. He paid for the room for one week. He had not eaten for several hours and asked the desk clerk where he could get something to eat this late at night. The desk clerk told him; only the saloons were open this late at night but some of them served food at all hours.

After getting his bags settled in his room he walked down the street. Saloons and bordellos were everywhere. People were moving about the city as if it were mid day instead of midnight. As Charlie walked down the street he looked into some of the saloons. Most of them were crowded with cowboys, gamblers and dance hall girls. He continued on down the street and walked around the corner of a building. There in a darkened alley he saw two men beating another and taking something from his pockets. He yelled at them and they looked up, dropped the man to the ground and ran. Charlie's cries had brought people out of the saloon and some one called the marshal.

As the marshal knelt by the injured man, he whispered the names of his assailants to him. Then several men carried him to the doctor's office where he died several hours later.

The marshal questioned Charlie. He told him his name and that he had arrived in town on the 11:00 P.M. train. Charlie described what he had seen.

The marshal knew the two men the dying man had named. They had a reputation as troublemakers and a long history of minor scrapes with the law. But nothing they could be sent to prison for until now. They were members of a large family from just outside town, who preferred to make trouble instead of work.

By 10:00 A.M. the next morning the marshal had arrested the two men and had them in jail. He asked Charlie to come to the jail and identify them. When he did so, the prisoners made threats and bragged about what their family would do if they were convicted.

Charlie was uncomfortable with the threats. The marshal assured him that the family did a lot of boasting and bragging. He told Charlie not to leave town until he could testify at the trial, which would be held in about three months.

Charlie found work and settled into getting acquainted with the city. He liked the scenery with the beautiful mountains and snowcapped peaks. The crisp cool climate agreed with him and he was soon felling better. He wrote letters to Laura describing how beautiful the country was. At first he did not tell Laura about the murder he had witnessed. But before the trial was to begin he wrote to her telling her about the murder and that as soon as the trial was finished he would be coming home.

As time grew near for the trial on several occasions Charlie had the feeling he was being followed. He could never see anyone but the feeling persisted. A few days before the trial was to begin Charlie did not show up for work. On the second day when he was not there his foreman went to the hotel to see if he had checked out. The desk clerk did not remember seeing Charlie for the past two days. He sent for the marshal and they went to Charlie's room.

They found him there, lying on the bed. He was dead. There were no signs of a struggle and no evidence of wounds to the body. The marshal ruled the death from natural causes. From the desk clerk he got the name of the next of kin and sent a telegram.

Polk Crabtree was in town when the telegram arrived. The telegraph operator saw him coming out of the general store and hurried over with the message. Polk was shocked. He hurried home to tell Laura. He walked into the little cabin where Laura was feeding baby Roy. The look on his face told Laura something was wrong. Polk could not say the words. He just handed the telegram to Laura. She stared at the telegram as if she did not understand the message. She handed the baby to Polk and started to the door. She took a few steps and collapsed in great wracking sobs.

Polk sent Perry to get Laura's mother and the Street family. When everyone arrived Polk showed the telegram to Ben. Salina began to tremble but no tears would come at this time.

Benjamin and Polk took the wagon back to town and telegraphed the marshal in Denver to send Charlie's body back to Arkansas for burial.

Polk, Laura, Benjamin and Salina met the train the day Charlie's body arrived. Several men were gathered at the depot and helped load the coffin onto the wagon. They took Charlie's body back to Benjamin's house. The next morning before they were to leave for the cemetery Benjamin and Laura opened the coffin lid. Laura looked on the face of Charlie for the last time. She had to be sure it was really Charlie and that he was really dead. It seemed incredible that at the age of thirty he could be dead from natural causes.

. As the family gathered at the cemetery, Salina barely heard the hymns or the eulogy. Pain inside her chest was so great she could hardly breath. The service ended and with heavy hearts the family left for home.

Baby Roy was not quite two years old when he died in June of 1914. He was laid to rest beside his father.

FIFTEEN

In 1915 Jay and Benjamin moved the log house further up the hill and built a frame home. He had fulfilled promise to Salina that someday she would have a proper house again. He built a home with four rooms down stairs and a small tower room on top and a porch across the front.

Although, Salina loved the house she did not like the fact that Benjamin had made a loan to build it. She had never liked owing money to anyone and for the first time in a very long time she thought of the home in Indiana.

Dorothy and Ruth played together and were more like sisters than cousins. One day while they were playing down by the creek they found a large flat rock secluded on three sides by bushes. They claimed this as their special place and promised never to tell anyone about it. They did not know it was the same place Carrie and Lillie had discovered when they had first arrived in Arkansas so many years ago.

The Great World War began in 1917. Jay registered for the draft and then volunteered. They rejected him because he was thirty-two years old with a wife and two children. Carrie was relieved.

One Saturday night in the summer of 1918 a dance was being held at one of the neighbors home. Fiddlers were playing and several couples were square dancing. Two young men came into the barn where people were dancing. They stood around for a while just watching. No one seemed to know them. But some of the men offered them drinks and tried to make conversation with them. The newcomers had little to say. Around 9:00 P.M. one of the men left the dance. A short time later he came back with two other men. The two newcomers pulled guns on the crowd and ordered the women and children outside. They gathered the men in one corner of the barn and held guns on them. The first two men grabbed Jay from the crowd of men.

Jay's Irish temper got the better of him and he began to fight both men. He was holding his own with the two of them until one of them grabbed him from behind and pinned his arms behind his back. Just then the man in front of him pulled a knife and slashed Jay's face and throat. As the blood spurted from Jay's neck they threw him to the floor and ran from the barn. Horses were heard galloping away.

No one knew why the men chose Jay as their victim. Was he chosen at random or had they held a grudge from some incident in the past? No one knew. Not even Jay.

The women and children rushed back into the barn. Carrie saw Jay lying in a pool of blood. The color drained from her face and she was almost as pale as Jay.

The men carried Jay into the house and placed him on a bed. The women brought ointments and bandages and helped Carrie clean and dress the wounds. Throughout the night Carrie sat by Jay's bed and watched as the blood oozed from his wounds. Finally as dawn was breaking the bleeding slowed and finally stopped. Carrie breathed a sigh of relief. Jay's breathing was so shallow and rapid. He was so pale. He looked as if he had no blood left.

Dorothy and Howard were cared for by some of the other women. They were so afraid their dad would die, but they had finally fallen asleep. In the morning Carrie woke them and told them their dad would be okay.

Around noon Jay's condition was stable. They laid him in the back of a wagon and took him to Benjamin and Salina's. Jay and Carrie stayed there for three weeks while Jay's wounds healed and he grew stronger.

Shortly after the attack several men had gone to notify the sheriff. He came the next day to question Jay and the other men who had been present. No one seemed to know who the men were or why they had attacked Jay. He was sure he had never seen them before.

Early in the morning following the attack, four men hopped a slow moving freight train as it came through Williford and were never seen again.

After that Jay and Carrie never attended dances.

SIXTEEN

In June of 1920 Jay and Carrie were living on Bridge Street in Jonesboro. Carrie had received a letter from Salina saying that Benjamin wasn't well. She wrote asking them to come and stay with her and Jay for a while so Benjamin could see a doctor there. Polk drove them to the depot in Williford and Jay met them in Jonesboro.

Benjamin saw a doctor who gave him medicine for a heart condition. In a few days Benjamin was feeling some better.

About 11:00 A.M. each morning Benjamin and Howard would go for a walk. Howard loved the time he spent with his grandfather.

On the morning of July 9th, Howard returned from playing with the neighborhood boys. He was eager to walk downtown with his grandfather. He found Benjamin on the front porch seated in a straight chair, leaning back against the wall, with his hat pulled down over his face. Howard gently touched him and called to him. When there was no response he ran into the house to get his mother and grandmother.

"Mama, come quick something is wrong with grandpa." Salina, Carrie and Dorothy ran to the porch. They found Benjamin still sitting in his chair. His life had slipped away while he slept.

Carrie's screams brought the neighbors. They called the police and then called the coroner. Someone went to get Jay.

Jay sent telegrams to Will and the girls in Indiana, and to Lillie in Oklahoma. He also sent one to Laura. She still lived in the little house Charlie had built for her when they were first married, even though she had married Charlie Darnell a few years earlier.

Two days later the family boarded the train to accompany Benjamin's body for the journey back to Williford. They arrived in Williford and went to the home of Jay's brother Dick Beavers and his wife, Effie. They would spend the night there and then go on to the cemetery tomorrow. Salina was numb. She had hardly spoken. Jay was worried about her. Carrie had not stopped crying since they had found Benjamin. The children spoke in low voices and had worried looks on their faces.

Howard had fun playing with his cousins Bill and Don. They played in the creek in front of the house and climbed on the rocks. His world seemed normal until he returned to the house and saw the coffin of his grandfather resting on the sawhorses in the parlor.

People came and went through out the evening, paying their final respects to a friend.

The next morning Polk and Laura arrived with Polk's wagon. They placed the coffin in the wagon and again the family started for the cemetery.

Salina could not believe it had been nineteen years since they had made the same journey with John. As they passed the homestead tears slid down her cheeks but no sound came from her.

Benjamin was laid to rest in the same row as Charlie and his children, with a place reserved for Salina. She had always hoped she would go first. She did not want to be the one left behind.

Aaron and Beth McKay and their children were at the funeral. Salina had not seen them for many years. Michael was twenty-two years old now with a wife and baby about the age he had been when he had traveled on the wagon train from Indiana.

Aaron and Beth had prospered and always remembered the journey to a new life, they had made with Benjamin and Salina.

After the funeral the family returned to Jonesboro and packed their belongings and moved back to the homestead. They lived there for a while but things were never the same without Benjamin.

Jay went to Oklahoma and worked with Jesse in the oil fields for a while. But he missed his family and soon returned home.

Salina lived the last ten years of her life with Carrie and Jay. After a time, they left the homestead and never again lived there. During the Great Depression they moved several times for Jay to find work.

In 1930 they were living near Hazen, Arkansas when Salina passed away late one Saturday afternoon. Once again the family gathered at the Baker Cemetery as Salina was laid to rest beside Benjamin.

Carrie's world again was devastated, when in 1932 word came that Lillie had died from pneumonia. She had never felt so alone before. Jay and Dorothy and Howard tried to console her but it would be a long time before she would feel her world was secure again.

Carrie and Jay moved many times in their lifetime, but the only place Carrie ever really thought of, as home was the homestead in the hills.

ABOUT THE AUTHOR

Darlene Martin grew up in north Arkansas not far from where Benjamin and Salina Street homesteaded land in 1898. She lived in central Illinois for many years and graduated from Illinois Central College with a degree in Registered Nursing. In 1992 she moved back to north Arkansas and now lives in the last home Jay and Carrie Beavers owned. She retired from the nursing profession in 2000 and now devotes her time to writing.

Darlene always remembered the stories her grandmother Carrie had told her and had hoped someday to write them down for future generations. In 1996 with retirement approaching she began writing *A Place to Call Home*. The novel is partly fiction but is based on her grandmother's stories. She has begun work on a second novel that she hopes to complete next year.

CPSIA information can be obtained
at www.ICGtesting.com
Printed in the USA
LVHW041737150623
749659LV00026B/556/J

9 781410 707178